WE MEET AGAIN

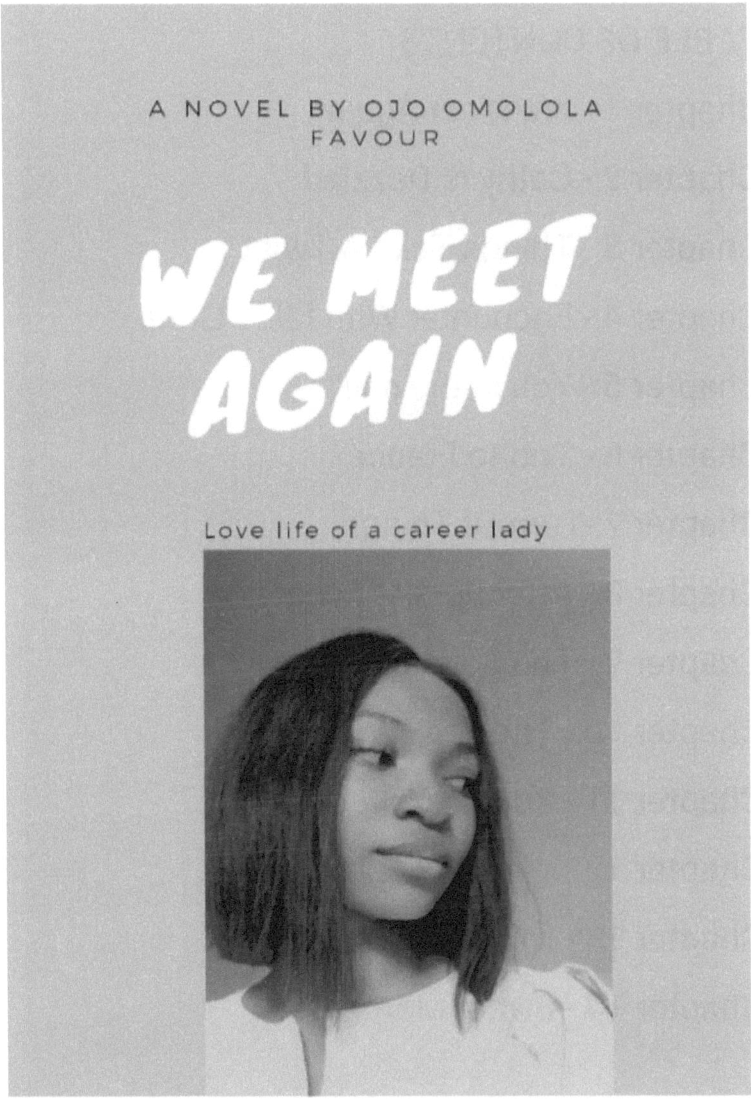
A NOVEL BY OJO OMOLOLA FAVOUR
WE MEET AGAIN
Love life of a career lady

TABLE OF CONTENTS

CHAPTER 1

WE MEET AGAIN

It was on a rainy night, Cathy was heading home from work. Then suddenly it began to rain, there was a convenience store nearby, she stopped by to get an umbrella. She got in and saw a young man eating noodles, she looked at him well and saw it was James, her long time crush from high school. She was so fascinated upon seeing him. They greeted each other and started to talk. James didn't get to eat anything throughout the day as he was busy with work. Cathy was unhappy seeing him that way. Not long after, the rain stopped. Cathy told him where she was headed and they happened to be living in the same neighborhood. They talked about how they've been throughout the years and the work they're doing. Cathy worked as a financial analyst, while James is also a financial analyst and a successful businessman. Cathy was the type that loved work, it's her major priority, and James happened to be the same. She's been counted as an ace in the company she worked for her smartness and brilliant memory. James was one of the directors in his company. They're in the same sector but work in different companies. They exchanged contacts and went to their homes. Cathy couldn't sleep easily that night, then she started to work on some of the tasks assigned to her.

Cathy's feelings for James remained the same, but he has no affection for her. James childhood friend, Mary, worked in the same company as him. They had always been matched as a couple because of the way they handle matters involving the topic, they're ace workers and co directors who got along so well. Mary liked him right from time because they grew up together, she gave up on being an artist and studied the same course as him. To her, it was love. Their background were similar as well. James happened to have some affections for Mary and he tried dating her. Their relationship progressed smoothly. But they're both workaholics, so they didn't get to spend much time with each other. They talk mainly about work when they're in the office, and then discussed about themselves when they're out. Mary wanted more attention than she was willing to offer, James wasn't that type, so it resolved into some issues between them.

A TV station interviewed James and then asked him some questions relating to work and his personal life. Cathy was at the cafe when she saw him on screen. The interviewer asked about his dating life and he has someone already,

Mary. Of course Mary was a known figure too, smart and beautiful. James had always been most ladies dream guy. Cathy felt sad upon hearing it, but she was a strong lady and got herself over it. She said to herself "if he's for me, then he'll definitely be mine".

On Cathy's way from work that night, she didn't get a bus or taxi as it was already late. She had resolved into trekking, but the place is quite far from her house. She sat at the bus stop, debating on whether to go back to work and then leave for home early the next day. A car parked in front of her, and a handsome young man came out and asked her for direction. He asked her what she's still doing there by that time of the night. Cathy could be sharp mouthed too, she answered "if I weren't here, would you have been able to find someone who's gonna help you with directions?". The guy apologized, and she just smiled. The man introduced himself as Chris and she told him her name also, Cathy. The guy offered to help her in return and drive her home. Upon telling him her address, they happened to be going the same way. The guy was jovial, so it made it an enjoyable drive for the both of them. They talked like they had known each other before. He dropped Cathy at her house and they exchanged contacts before he left.

Chris and Cathy got along quite well, and he started picking her up from work every day. Her colleagues started to think he's her boyfriend, but she didn't tell them if they're dating or not. They developed feelings for each other slowly. Chris confessed his feelings to her, but she said to take things slowly. Cathy had not been in a relationship before, and she wasn't ready for such yet. Chris understood her and waited for her. They opened up to each other about what they desired in a mate.

There was a conference on finance, which involved every finance companies attending. Different companies hosted it every year, it was Cathy's company to host it. Cathy was selected as one of the speakers, and she played her part well. James who was in attendance was mesmerized by her, her beauty, posture, confidence, and speech. Him and Cathy were only classmates who knew nothing or little about each other. He started to think about her. Ever since he began dating Mary, he already forgot about her. He was curious to know more and more things about Cathy. He started to think if he has feelings for her, and if it's possible for him to like two women. Mary, his girlfriend, liked him from childhood and gave up on being an artist and studied the same course as him. She had always drew photos of him. He was wondering if the affection he had for her was a brotherly affection. It got him confused.

CHAPTER 2

CATHY IS DAZZLED

At TEB where Cathy worked, the acquisition of a proposed project didn't go well. The company had invested much funds and was going bankrupt already. Some employees were fired, leaving a few staff behind. The work load on the remaining employees became tedious. She had to work overtime, and draft proposals. As the head of a team, she had to meet with some investors, but no one was willing to offer help. The CEO and board of directors weren't settled, as they were looking for means out. They called series of meetings which led to no progress. At MLT, where James worked, the CEO Bryan took measures to purchase TEB. The two companies have always had equal strength, it was hard for them as Bryan continuously sent proposals. They later resolved into merging and TEB became under MLT. Cathy was transferred to the branch where James worked. She wasn't a team leader anymore as she was degraded into an assistant that worked under Mary. It wasn't easy for her, though she was a strong woman. The rules are different from TEB's, the work also. Mary recognized her efforts and recommended her for promotion. Chris hasn't been hearing from Cathy recently, he felt she was busy, and had forgotten about him. While he was thinking about her, Cathy called him. He happily picked the call, she told him about her new job and how she was given promotion. Well, he was the only friend she had. Then they decided to celebrate it at a XL club. Cathy is the sexy office worker type of woman, she enjoyed partying. They scheduled it for 9pm and Chris agreed to pick her up by then. Cathy had no idea Chris was a musician, she thought he was a idle CEO or so. On that night at XL, as they entered, she noticed the way ladies were all over him, she wasn't comfortable with it, but put up with it. Chris excused himself, took the stage and sang a mind blowing song, he said it was dedicated to his friend Cathy. She felt moved, the people there turned their attention on her, wanting to see how she looks, she was dashing though. She had fun on that night and later went home around 11pm, Chris dropped her as usual. The next day was Saturday, she browsed the news all to see her pics taken with Chris at the club. She wasn't much bothered about it, she started her work. On Monday at the office, the workers were all looking at her with amusement, she ignored it, then went straight to her office. Rumors were already circulating that she was dating Chris and got her position due to connections. She happened to hear some junior staff talking about it, and she told them "if you think I got here due to my connections, then you can do the same". James relationship with Mary wasn't going smoothly. He could not put up with her overbearing attitude. He was thinking about trying things out with Cathy, but the rumors didn't let him. Cathy didn't respond to those rumors, it was no one's business whoever she chooses to date. During work break, she went to a nearby cafe to drink coffee and get some air, James happened to be there as well. On seeing her, he approached her, they both sat down to talk. He asked her about Chris, she said they were only friends. James felt assured in his mind. But Cathy had already started to like Chris and has no feelings for him any longer. It was ten minutes to the end of the break and she decided to leave, James offered to give her a ride since they were going the same way. The workers who saw her alight from his car, started to think she's connected to James too, which led to another rumors. He started to come to her office, as she's now a team leader to ask for her views on a particular issue. Some workers said she's started to date James and has left Chris. Some said well Chris is in the music industry, he probably doesn't know what's going on with her. Mary started to feel jealous and disliked Cathy. She looked into her information and found out she was former classmates with James. Cathy was pretty and smart, and a powerful opponent to her. The company rumors continued. Some employees began to like Cathy and took her as a role model. They all began to think she was more appropriate for James than Mary.

Cathy called Chris to meet up during weekend. They talked about how the week went for them. She felt relaxed conversing with him and enjoyed his company. Chris asked her if there's anything she does for fun apart from clubbing, and she said she doesn't, so he taught her to how play games. She won him quite a few times, she was good at calculating things. Chris left at night, she was left alone and began to think. She had always weighed and compared things before reaching a decision. She felt happy when she was with Chris, compared with James, so it got her wondering what she feels for him, and maybe it's because he's her first friend ever. She couldn't do anything that night and decided to arrange her books in her study. She stumbled on a book and opened it, inside it was a note: "Two people who are too similar is just like two parallel lines. It's hard to intersect. They should find someone who complements them with intersection just like "perfect" and "casual". Even if they have different starting points, and direction in life, it's like climbing a mountain. Be willing to wait for him or her halfway up the mountain. Take their hand and be with them." These words made her think that she and James are similar in their pursuit and can't be together, She was hoping of getting to know Chris better.

CHAPTER 3

THINGS TAKE A TWIST

At MLT, Cathy's office.

Cathy was assigned a project, which really mattered to the company. It was to be done perfectly without any information leaked. She started working on it and was gathering necessary information. Mary heard about it from her and was unhappy. She thought hard about what to do, she wanted her out from the company. She called one of her loyal team members, Steve, who was good at installing cameras, and told him she wanted him to help her fix a camera close to Cathy's desk. When everyone had left for home, Steve carried out his operation, and fixed the camera. It was positioned in such a way that it's opposite Cathy's desk. He connected the camera to Mary's system, she could see whatever Cathy's doing on her computer. The project was to be handed in at the board's meeting in two days. Cathy finished it a day before the appointed time. Mary copied her work and sent it to their rival company, BM finance. The CEO was her brother, Mary stayed at MLT only because of James. The public didn't pay too much attention on her, because they thought MLT and BM finance will reach an agreement someday.BM finance had not been on good terms with MLT, as it has always been opposing it. The two companies were competing for the project too. At the board meeting, Cathy presented her project and was making some illustrations, it was going smoothly, then suddenly news surfaced online as BM finance proposes the project too. It was a shock to everyone, as they thought Cathy copied the ideas or leaked the information, the matter was unclear. They dismissed the meeting and scheduled an urgent one for the next day, their chances of winning against BM finance was low. Cathy was suspended from work as the company started interrogation, she was despaired not knowing what to do, it was the first time she was experiencing such. If she ends up being fired, she'd have to pay compensation too. There was no way to prove her innocence. She called James and discussed with him, but he didn't seem to believe her or anything. He didn't want to get involved in the matter. The she called Chris and told him about the matter, then he suggested to check the company's security footage. The strange part of it was that only a part of the project was copied, not all. The security footage was checked, a CCTV camera was installed in every office. It was found that Steve had sneaked into her office and installed a camera. She went to James and told him about it, they checked her office and found the camera. James confirmed that the camera was Steve's doing. It was the

CCTV footage that made him pay attention to Cathy, he was merely concerned about his position. Steve was summoned and interrogated, he couldn't give a valid answer as he tried to protect Mary. The issue remained unclear and there was no hint, Steve was arrested by the police to make their findings. They treated it as the company's internal affair and didn't want the public's attention on it. But there was no better option than letting the police make their findings. Steve was working under Mary, so a search warrant was issued to check the department where he worked. They couldn't take a look at their systems for the sake of the company's privacy. Mary went into her office and opened a folder mistakenly on her system, it was where the copied information was. A call came in and she had to excuse herself. The police were still making the search when one of the junior staff took a look at Mary's system and said "isn't this the leaked project". That drew everyone's attention and they saw it. Mary came in not long after, the police interrogated her. She gave in and told them the truth, she knew she had lost already. Mary was dismissed from the company, and Steve was fired. James relationship with Mary ended as well because of the incidence. Cathy was called to resume the following week. There was still four days left to a Monday, Cathy was bored at home. She couldn't do much work from home, and used the chance to get a good rest. Chris came visiting during evening, they both talked and he congratulated her on proving her innocence and keeping her job.

Cathy went out with Chris on Saturday night and took some drinks with him. She got drunk and then told him about her feelings. Cathy didn't have alcohol tolerance. Chris felt happy and told her he loves her in return. She added that she was grateful for the fact that he was by her during those moments, it gave her the strength to keep going. Their relationship started on that day. He took Cathy to her home and then left. Cathy woke up the next morning and remembered what she said to Chris, she felt a bit embarrassed but settled. Chris call entered, he asked how she is and told her he's traveling for a show and would be away for two days. He told her not to miss him too much that he'll be back soon.

Chris checked in at the De Great hotel, he happened to meet his ex girlfriend Alex, who also lodged there. They exchanged pleasantries and was photographed together. News surfaced online that Chris and his model ex girlfriend are back together. Cathy saw it, but was having the feeling that it's not true. He only told her he was traveling for a show. Chris returned in two days as he promised, and went to see Cathy. She asked him if the rumors were true, and he said no that they only happened to see each other and Alex was invited to the show as well.

Alex mother had heart failure and required surgery. Her mum saw the news and thought her daughter was back with Chris for real. She really liked him. Alex told her they were back, so she won't be worried. She called Chris and pleaded with him to tell her mum that they're dating . She explained the situation to him and told him she'll tell her mum the truth when she recovers. He agreed to do it. Chris didn't tell Cathy about it, as he didn't want to make her sad. He started visiting Alex mum at the hospital and didn't have much time for his girlfriend anymore. Cathy was worried about him, but after some days, she didn't bother him and focused on her work.

Cathy's sister put to bed in the hospital Alex Mum's was admitted to. Cathy was called and went over to see her. On getting there, she saw Chris and Alex standing outside a room, Alex Mum's was undergoing surgery. She walked up to them and asked Alex what they're doing there and how she's related to Chris. She said they were dating and her mum is undergoing surgery. Then she faced Chris and asked if it was true, he only apologized to her. Cathy walked away and went to see her sister, she congratulated her and then excused herself. On getting out, Chris was standing by the door, he held her hand to stop her from leaving and tried to explain things. Cathy wasn't willing to, she said she wanna be left alone. She went outside and took some fresh air. She listened to a podcast on relationship and took note of these words: "If everyone can be together while being in love, there won't be so many unmarried or single men and women in this world, and there won't be any rows and reconciliations."

CHAPTER 4

ENCOUNTER WITH MISS LINDA

Cathy sat outside thinking deeply and was heartbroken. She didn't feel at ease so she decided to take a stroll. She saw an elderly man in his 70s trying to pick a book that fell from him, so she walked towards him and helped him pick it. The man thanked her and asked for her name, she said she's Cathy. He went ahead and asked why she was looking so sad, she didn't wanna say it, but the man pressed on her, so she narrated it to him. Cathy asked in return what he was doing there, seeing he was wearing a patient's uniform, he said he's recuperating after the surgery he undergone. The man told her he had a daughter just like her, whose name is Linda and she'd be visiting by 7pm. He asked if she'd be available to meet her and she said she'll try. She added that her sister just gave birth so she'll still be around till the next day, before her sister gets discharged. The man said he was hungry, so she helped him to get some food and told him she'll see him around 7pm that she wants to go and check on her sister. She asked for his hospital room and then left for the ward where her sister was. Chris met her on her way back and stopped her, he said he wants to have a discussion with her, but Cathy left saying there's nothing to talk about. He went after her and said it was a misunderstanding. Cathy replied that it wasn't, and she wouldn't believe such. She believed him at first, but she's not gonna do that this time around. Chris was begging her to hear him out, but she turned a deaf ear to it and walked away. On getting to the room where her sister was, she asked Cathy where she had been. Cathy told her, and her sister asked if she's here to see her or somebody else. Cathy replied saying she actually came there for her, and she happened to meet Chris with a girl, then met a man whom she made appointment with. She told her sister what happened between her and Chris and how she felt. Her sister said to hear him out before reaching a conclusion and she said she's not willing to, so her sister told her just to follow her mind. But she should remember that she's of marriageable age and get on with someone who's sincere and loves her.

Cathy went to the room where the man was around 7pm. She saw a beautiful young lady by him, she greeted them both and the lady replied warmly. The man introduced the lady to her saying this is Linda, my daughter I told you about. He introduced Cathy to Linda as well. Linda said she wants to get something and asked if Cathy can accompany her. She agreed and they walked out of the room. Chris met them outside and asked for a conversation with Cathy, but she turned him down. Chris had remained in the hospital because of her, and doesn't know what to do anymore. Linda asked what's going on and Cathy said to ignore. Then Linda said that's he's so goodlooking and looks nice, why does she not want to talk to him. Cathy replied if he's so goodlooking, you can have him to yourself, well I'm not interested. Linda replied, really can I? Cathy asked are we out here to get something or too woo a man? Linda said it's both, Cathy casted a stern look at her, and Linda smiled saying she was only kidding her. But since she likes him, why can't she try to hear him out. Cathy told her to mind her business that some things are best not known. Linda told her not to regret if she wins him over. She added that he looks like a singer and Cathy replied he's the one. Linda said it's gonna be awesome having a popular and handsome guy that she's always been his fan, and didn't know she'd get to see him this way. Cathy felt jealous and said to do what she wants. Linda sensed it and said she was only kidding her, but on a serious note, she should look beyond her emotions and try to know the situation. She added that her dad already told her about Cathy's situation, and she used the excuse of getting something to speak with her as a woman to woman. She said she's a great reader just like her dad and she's somewhat experienced when it comes to relationship. She's a conversationalist and and a counselor, she did the talk on relationship during noon which Cathy listened to the podcast. Cathy said she thought that her voice sounded familiar, Linda replied that she's the one, and also has bookshops. Cathy was surprised and felt relieved to talk with her, she opened up to her on her feelings for Chris. Linda told her "no matter the situation, never let your emotions overpower your intelligence". Cathy took note of those words and thanked her. Linda said to listen to him and find out what happened, whether Chris was real or not. And even if he wasn't real to her, since he seemed to care, she can win him over. She added that he's a popular guy with a lot of girls around him, it's normal for rumors to spread, but she should trust him that's he's a sincere type. But Chris must have proven himself before she can trust him. And if she finds out that he isn't real, she should let him be to prevent further heartbreak. Cathy felt comforted by those words, Linda hugged her. They went to a mall and bought some things and returned to the hospital. On their way back, they were in a gist about work and other things, Cathy felt happy. They went to see Linda's dad, Cathy bid them goodbye and returned to her sister's ward.

CHAPTER 5

YOU'RE THE ONE

Cathy went to sister's ward and told her she was leaving, so she can prepare for tomorrow's work. Her sister asked her to stay, but she said it'd be inconvenient for her. Her sister's husband came in, they exchanged greetings and she congratulated him. She turned to her sister and said "you see your husband is here already, can you let go of me now". Her sister laughed and she can leave now, Cathy went to see the baby, she was sleeping already, she smiled at her and said goodnight. Her sister said she didn't spend much time with her, Cathy said not to worry and that she'd be spending the weekend with her. She said she might not be there to send her home tomorrow after she gets discharged, but her brother in law would handle that. Her sister's husband replied that it's his responsibility and she should find a husband too and get congratulated. Cathy's sister said she had reminded her of that and should stop delaying everyone, they all wants to see her get married. Cathy said she won't let them down and left.

Cathy saw Chris downstairs, she went to meet him and asked what he was still doing there. He said he was waiting for her, Cathy felt pity for him and told him she was leaving already. Chris asked if he could drive her home and she said no. He persuaded her and she agreed. While they were about to leave, Alex came near and asked why Chris was leaving, he didn't ask how her mum was doing and was just following Cathy around. Chris replied that he had already done her the favor by lying that he was her boyfriend when they're no longer dating. Cathy looked at him confused. Chris added that she already ruined his relationship by saying that they were dating, she knew Cathy was his girlfriend and said that to her. And now, how should he prove himself. Alex felt angry at turned to Cathy that Chris left her because of Cathy. Cathy replied that whatever happened between them is none of her concern and next time she should know how to keep her possessions safe. Chris held Cathy's hand and they left. When they got to the parking lot, and reached where Chris car was, she removed her hand from his. Chris only smiled a little, they got In and he drove off. Chris didn't take Cathy to her house, he took her to another place that had a nice scenery, it was along the road. Cathy asked what they were doing there and he said he wants to tell her some things that has always been on his mind. He held her hand and saw her bracelet, he looked at it well and asked if that's what she was putting on before or just wore it that night. Cathy said that she hardly wears it, and it's the first time she wore it since they both met. She added that she's putting on a shirt, maybe the sleeve covered it. Chris looked at her with amusement, she asked why he was looking at her that way. He said he doesn't know what to say anymore, Cathy asked how can that be, and did he not say that he had some things to tell her. Chris lifted his sleeve a little and showed her his bracelet too, it was exactly the same, it was old fashioned but the two bracelets are a pair, they both had C inscribed on it. Chris asked if she remembered the place they both were, she said she doesn't. He said he brought her there just to tell her his story of how he met a teenage girl who helped him when we was younger, and though they couldn't meet again, but he has always seen Cathy as the one. Her smile, voice and hair color were similar to the girl's own. He was involved in a car accident with his parents some years back on their way home at night, they went out to celebrate his birthday. They ran into a truck, an accident occured, the windscreen broke, their car was compressed, and his parents died. He was sitting at the back, the glass entered his body as well and was bleeding, there was no one to help as there were no passers by or vehicles. Then a girl was approaching where he was, she looked through and saw him. There was no way she could help him as well, she called emergency number and saw a damaged metal chair along the road. She used it and broke the car glass and helped him come out, he didn't know he could do such and realized people become strong through circumstances. The girl had two bracelets on and gave him one. She sympathized with him and consoled him regarding his loss. He asked why she helped him, she smiled a little and said God has a purpose for your life, so he kept you alive. An ambulance arrived not long after and carried him. His parents corpse were taken away as well. And that word has been a strong motivation for him. When he recovered after some days, he went looking for her, but couldn't find her, so kept her bracelet hoping they'd meet one day.

Cathy was shocked upon hearing that, and was moved to tears, she checked his wrist and saw a glass cut there. The cut resulted when she broke the car's window. She said she had forgotten all of these before and just remembered it. She said it's no wonder he felt familiar to her. She said that she came visiting her uncle for holiday then and left the next day. But she had always had him in mind and prayed that God keeps him safe wherever he is. She said where he brought her to was where the accident occured, Chris replied yes. Chris went on and apologized to her. He said he was sorry for not recognizing her, he was sorry for hiding things from her, and hurting her feelings. He wasn't thoughtful enough and caused the misunderstanding. Cathy said she's forgiven him, not because of what happened between them years back, but because of his persistence, she doesn't like being bothered. Chris smiled and hugged her, Cathy said he should always be honest about his feelings and shouldn't do such anymore. She said she's not gonna tolerate such, and doesn't know why she's kind to him. Chris replied that it's because they are fated, she didn't reply him and just looked at him. They left the place, stopped by an eatery and bought some food, then he took her home.

CHAPTER 6

TRIP TO FRANCE

Cathy returned to work on Monday, she sat in her office when a call came in through the office telephone. It was Ann, the CEO's secretary, she told Cathy that the CEO wants to see her urgently. Cathy left for the CEO's office, on getting there, she saw James seated as well. The CEO, Bryan asked her to take her sit, he said there's an urgent project that he wants the both of them to handle, he has purchased their tickets and they should prepare to leave for France the next day. Bryan dismissed them and Cathy left, when James was about to leave, he called him back and said it's a chance for him to get along with Cathy. Mary is no longer there, and Cathy seems to be the best choice, he should make the project a success also. James replied he won't let him down and left. Cathy called Chris when she got to her office and told him about her work trip to France. Chris said it's alright and would pick her up in the evening.

Chris showed up at MLT during evening and stood at the reception, he called Cathy who said she's on her way. The female staff were surprised and happy to see him, including the male staff, they requested for his autograph and were wondering what he was doing there. They knew he was there for Cathy though, but don't know what's going on between them exactly. Cathy approached Chris and they left. She told him that he's leaving with James, and Chris said it's alright that she had told him before, he told her to be careful. When they got to Cathy's house, he helped her pack her belongings and told her to get a good rest, he left not long after.

Cathy met with James at the airport the next day, they boarded the plane together and chatted as the plane took off, she had turned her phone off. They talked mainly about work, then he asked about Chris, Cathy smiled and said they're doing well, and they plan to announce their relationship after some time. James wasn't quite happy about it, Cathy asked about Mary and he replied that they broke up. Cathy said ohh and took a nap. They arrived at the airport and they got off, they boarded a taxi and lodged at an hotel, they took different rooms. Cathy called Chris that she's settled already. James came knocking on the door and she let him in. He asked if she was fine, and she said she is. Cathy didn't feel comfortable being alone in a room with him and told him she wants to get some rest and they'll meet later during evening. James said okay and left. Cathy took a rest and reviewed some documents that was sent to her. Cathy met with James during evening at the bar, he told her they'll be visiting SLC tomorrow and she said okay. They discussed about other things as well, James noticed that she enjoyed talking about Chris, as she kept mentioning him.

Chris had posted Cathy's picture online, though she was unaware and his friends commented she's a beautiful hardworking lady. Tony, Chris childhood friend, happened to be at the same bar where Cathy and James was. He chatted Chris and asked him to send his girlfriend's photo, he did and Tony compared the photo with Cathy. Chris called Tony and asked what's up, he said he saw a lady chatting happily with a man, she seemed familiar and found out that she's Cathy. Chris said that his girlfriend is in France with James her co worker for a work trip, what would she be doing at the bar this late. Tony replied that he'll send photos if Chris doesn't believe him. Tony took photos of James and Cathy, they were chatting and drinking together. He approached them and said they look nice together, it's lovely to date someone with similar vibe. James smiled, and Cathy said they're co workers. Tony laughed and introduced himself, Cathy and James introduced themselves in turn. Tony asked if they could take pictures together and they agreed, he took a picture of the three of them and left. Tony sent the photos to Chris, he felt somehow about it and told his friend that he's not gonna ask Cathy about it until she arrives, he doesn't want her to be distracted. He added that they aren't supposed to be alone in such place though they're co workers, it can cause a misunderstanding. Tony replied that he should make sure that James don't get too close to his girlfriend and he's up to something.

Cathy and James visited SLC the following day, they met with the director and they discussed about the project. The director, Andre doesn't want to allocate the project to MLT because some shareholders didn't agree to it. Cathy showed him the proposal that she drafted, Andre read it and asked her to send it to his email and come back by 3pm that the company wants to hold a meeting. At SLC's meeting room, Andre talked about MLT's proposal and the shareholders reviewed it. They said it was better than the other company they wanted to cooperate with, so they agreed with MLT. The meeting ended and he called Cathy, she showed up with James and Andre told them that the shareholders agreed to it. They were about to give it out to another company, but he's happy that they got to collaborate with MLT. He said MLT has a nice reputation and there's many chances of success with it. James replied that MLT has been wanting the project for long, before they got involved with it, and the CEO assigned the project to them after it was stated on the news that SLC will be cooperating with another company. Andre replied that he knew MLT wanted to collaborate with them, he assigned the project to them and they left. Cathy said she's happy that it's a success and they can return home on time. Cathy stopped by a store and bought some gifts for her sister and her baby, it was a baby girl, so she bought some nice clothes for her niece. She bought a wristwatch for Chris as well and matching outfits. Chris call came in and she told him her work trip was a success and will be returning the next day. Chris said it's a good news and he'll be expecting her. She went outside, took some photos and sent it to Chris. James went to meet Cathy and asked her when she intends to return home, she said tomorrow, he said it's fine and that they can leave together. He saw the stuff she was carrying and asked if she bought something for him, she said no but she can get it for him now. James said not to worry that she should just help him select something, he's paying. They went in, she helped him pick a tie and they left.

CHAPTER 7

TURN OF THINGS

Cathy returned the following day with James. They reported at work, and Cathy requested for a two days leave. Chris only knew she was arriving on that day, but he didn't know she has arrived. Cathy left work earlier than she used to and went to Chris home, she had his spare key. Chris was not around, and she prepared a meal for both of them while waiting for him. She dished the food In the warmer and slept on the couch. Chris wasn't back till around 9pm, he entered and was surprised to see her in his house, it was her first time of coming there. Cathy was still sleeping when a call came in through her phone, it woke her up and she picked it, it was her sister who called to check on her.

Chris said to Cathy that he's happy to see her and it's really surprising. Cathy replied that she only wanted to give him a surprise. Chris said that's it's thoughtful of her to do that. She said she's hungry and they should eat now. While eating, Chris looked like he had something to say. Cathy asked him what's up, he said there's nothing that she should continue eating. Cathy urged him and he said he really has nothing to say, he told Cathy to get a good rest after eating that she had travelled a long way. He stood up and went to his room, Cathy followed him and told him to stop acting strange and just talk to her. Chris looked at her and asked her what she did with James while she was away. She said they did nothing, and only had a work relationship. Chris said okay and showed her the pictures Tony sent to him, he asked why they're intimate and why she would be with him alone in such place. Cathy answered that she was only bored and there's nothing going on with them, she apologized to him and said she was at fault. Chris replied that he wasn't angry and just wanted her to know that it's wrong of her to behave that way. He said that he trusted her, but it's hard for another person to believe there's nothing going on between her and Chris. He told her to be careful and won't be tolerating such, Cathy nodded. Chris said it's late and she should sleep on time because of work, Cathy replied that she's on leave. Chris said to listen to him play a song then, he picked his guitar and sang one of his songs. Cathy told him it's nice and asked if it's a new song, he said yes and it's for her, Cathy smiled and said she was feeling sleepy. She went to bed, leaving him alone.

Cathy left Chris place the following day, she told him she

has some work to do and Chris dropped her. Cathy reviewed some documents and sent it to James. She met up with Linda the second day and asked how her dad is, Linda replied he's fine and has been discharged. Cathy told her about what happened to her and asked for her advice, Linda only told her to be careful in such matters and not get too involved with James. Linda said Chris is a man and he loves her, so it's normal of him to feel that way, and she doesn't feel he's angry about it, but only wanted her to know how he felt. Linda added that anyone could easily misunderstand her and recommended some books to her. She left not long after and returned home.

She returned to work after her leave has ended. She performed her tasks when a call came in through the office telephone, it was Ann, the CEO's secretary, he had requested to see her. She went to the CEO's office and he offered her a sit. The CEO, Bryan, commended her work and told her she's been promoted, and her promotion letter has been sent to her mail. She thanked him and left, she met James on her way to her office and exchanged greetings with him. He asked if they could meet up after work and she declined politely saying she has plans already. Cathy returned to her office and continued her work.

WE MEET AGAIN

The next day was a Saturday, Cathy sat at home reading a book, her mind wasn't settled as she had not heard from Chris. She decided to call him and asked what he's been up to, he said he was sorry for not checking on her that he's not been feeling well. Cathy told him that she'll check on him in the evening. Cathy went to see him as promised and looked after him, then a call entered through Chris phone, it was his ex girlfriend, Luna. Chris picked and asked her what's up, she said she's around and would like to pay him a visit. Chris told her that he has a new girlfriend now and it's not polite of her to visit him, but they can meet up elsewhere. Luna said it's okay and asked who his girlfriend is, he said he'd be announcing his relationship when it's time, but her name is Cathy by the way. Luna felt offended and hanged up, Chris turned to Cathy and said it's his ex, Luna. She asked if it's the popular actress and he said yes, so Cathy asked if he could tell him why they broke up. Chris replied that it was Luna who initiated the breakup and left him for another person, he was still struggling in his career then. He added that the guy Luna left him for was the one who backed her career and got her a reliable agency. However things didn't go smoothly between them though he was helping her, the guy loved to flirt and Luna can't endure such. Cathy asked that so she ended the relationship because of that, Chris replied yes. Cathy said that Luna stated it in her interview that she called off her relationship, because the guy wasn't devoted to her. But she faced some criticisms about why she only ended it when she's become famous, and was she not aware of his personality before. Cathy said, to others it seems she only used the man for her benefit, however her acting is good and she enjoys her movies. Chris said it's her personal life and it's up to her on how to manage her affairs. He said to talk about him and Cathy, when should they get married. Cathy asked if he was kidding, that they should get to know each other's family first. Chris asked if it's because he hasn't proposed to her yet, and she said it's not like that. Cathy then asked him if he knows why Luna wanted to see him, Chris answered no that he doesn't. Cathy asked what if she wants to reconcile with him, Chris replied it's not possible even if it's the case. Cathy asked why Chris has only celebrity ex girlfriends, he said maybe he was only interested in such ladies before meeting her. Cathy said it's okay and he should meet up with her to know what's on her mind. Chris asked if she's sending him to her, Cathy replied no and that there's nothing wrong in meeting up, he looked at her and didn't say a word. Cathy asked why is he not talking, he said there's nothing left to say after she had made a decision for him. He asked if she wasn't jealous and said there's nothing to be jealous about, after all she owns him. Chris smiled and asked to play games with her and she agreed.

CHAPTER 8

AFFECTIONATE EVENTS

Cathy returned to work on Monday, she did her work as usual. It was 2pm, the company's lunch break, she went to the company's canteen, and was already eating when she saw James approaching where she was seated with his food and sat opposite her. Cathy was a bit surprised to see him and they exchanged greetings. She asked him what he was doing there, and he said he came to eat of course. Cathy said it's rare for the MD to eat where everyone eats, James answered that as the managing director, he shouldn't eat elsewhere, and he can't possibly drink only coffee or stay hungry, he should promote the company. Cathy told him that eating in the company's canteen isn't enough, he should work harder and James replied he'd do his best. James stared at Cathy and she asked him what's going on, he said isn't she a director as well, why then is she talking about him. Cathy answered that her position is lower to his, James didn't reply her and focused on eating. Cathy asked James if he's in touch with Mary, he replied no, and that after the incident he hasn't heard anything about her. The break was over, a text came in through James phone, and he left hurriedly, Cathy was wondering why his countenance changed and why he had to leave so fast. Cathy left for her office, the company staff were staring at her, she ignored them and continued walking. Luna had an interview around 10am, the interviewer asked about her about her endorsement deal with Perfect Jewelry and she answered him. Then he asked her about her love life and she mentioned Chris. She said her and Chris were lovers but broke up as a result of their differences, they couldn't get used to each other and had continual misunderstandings which teared them apart, but they'll be back together soon as they're doing well. The interviewer said it's a good news, Luna smiled and said indeed it is. The interviewer asked if it's the popular musician, Chris, Luna answered yes. The interviewer was surprised and congratulated her, he said they're so compatible and would have a blessed future. Comments were flooding the Internet in the comment section after the video was posted online. Some said it's a good thing Luna will be settling down soon. Some said Chris is a playboy and has a lot of girlfriends, he dates celebrities mainly. Some said Chris is too good for her and Luna doesn't deserve him. Some said they're a great match and they're happy for them. Some said they'll make a lovely couple and they're awaiting their wedding. People were expressing their opinions under the comment section. Luna's interview video had went viral, and nearly everyone in the company had watched it. Some of the staff said that Cathy is only a toy to kill boredom to Chris, and that he's way out of her league. Others said she's a dreamer, and that Chris had never mentioned her to the public before. Some said she's only deceiving herself, Chris can't be serious with any lady, let alone Cathy, an unknown person. Some said she'd better avoid heartbreak by finding someone else, then one of the staff mentioned James, then they said James is a great match for her. Some said Chris might be serious with Cathy though, she's a beautiful and hardworking lady. Then one person mentioned Alex, one of Chris ex girlfriends; the person said that Chris could break up with a super model like Alex, who is Cathy compared to her. Others said they should watch how the story would turn out. Cathy reached her office, and picked some files on her desk, then she headed for her team members office. On getting there, she saw her assistant, Tracy, watching something on her phone, she didn't know what Tracy was watching. The team members were discussing about Luna's interview video that circulated the company, on seeing her, they stopped and reached for their computers. They greeted her except Tracy who was so focused on her phone, her colleagues wanted to tap her to let her know that their boss is around, but she stopped them, they were working under her. Cathy approached her, tapped her, and asked her what she was doing, Tracy was surprised on seeing her and turned off her phone's screen, she said she was doing nothing. Cathy looked at her and asked Tracy about the project she was handling, but she said she hasn't been able to gather much information and she's still working on it. Then Cathy asked her to hand her phone over that she wants to see what she was watching that took her attention, Tracy stared at her and gave her her phone, Cathy saw that it was Luna's interview video and gave Tracy her phone back, she said Tracy should only focus on work matters in the office. Tracy answered her that she won't do such anymore but she should watch till the end, so Cathy collected the video and watched it. She wasn't very shocked when she watched the part where Luna announced that she'll be with Chris soon, she returned Tracy's phone to her and told her to send every document pertaining the project to her and left. Her team members were looking at her as she left and was wondering what's going on in her mind. Cathy returned to her office, sat on her chair and leaned her head backwards, after resting on a while, she started working on her computer and was reviewing some documents.

Luna called Chris and asked if he was free that she wants to see him, Chris agreed and Luna said she'll text him the address. Chris went to Home Bites, a restaurant, and asked the waiter where Luna's dining room is, she rented a VIP dining space that contains only her table in the room, a waiter took him there and he saw Luna, they exchanged pleasantries and he sat down. Luna smiled at him and asked how he is, and he said he's doing fine, Chris asked Luna in return how she is and she replied she's doing well. Chris said it's obvious that she's well, he asked if she's in contact with her ex, and she said yes, and that he wants to come back to her but she's not interested in him. Chris asked why, Luna replied that the relationship was toxic and she's over him already, and now, the only person in her heart is Chris. Chris looked at her and said it's not possible, Luna asked why, he replied that he's in love with another lady and will be getting married soon. Luna said it can't be, she won Chris heart once, so she can do that again, Chris replied that he thought what he wanted in a woman was only her physical attraction and passion, but now, he's realized that he wants something more, he needs a woman that can stay by him, a woman that can understand him, and someone who handle her work while keeping her family in shape, that is someone who doesn't let her feelings interfere with her work. Luna held his hands that she can be that woman, Chris replied she can't, he added that sometimes, the best way to love someone is not possessing them, you should desire their happiness. Luna was trying to persuade him, Chris said no amount of pleading can work, a call entered through his phone while he was still talking. It was Tony, his friend residing in France, Chris picked him and asked him what's up, why did he have to call instead of dropping a message on his Whatsapp, Tony told him to check the Internet, there's news about him and Luna getting back together. Chris was shocked and opened his eyes wide, he looked at Luna in anger and told Tony that he'll call him back, he hanged up and check the Internet, he saw Luna's interview video, watched it and read the comments, Luna was looking down when Chris was going through his phone, she knew she had made Chris upset and could not look at him in the face. Chris and Luna was photographed at the dining space and the pictures was posted online too, Chris saw the pictures online and looked at the picture well, it was taken when he entered the room and shook hands with Luna, another shot was taken when he sat down and smiled at Luna. Chris said to Luna that those pictures were taken by the waiter who brought him in right, Luna replied no, that it might be another person who did it. Chris told Luna that she set him up on purpose in order to fulfill her wish, Luna begged him to play along in order to protect her name, Chris said he can't do that and he's not gonna hurt the woman he loves a second time, he left angrily after saying that. Luna had called some reporters before, because she thought she and Chris would be going out together and would be creating an impression that they're dating. On getting outside, Chris met some reporters, he ignored them and went towards his car, the reporters blocked his way and asked if it's true that he's dating Luna, and how long have they been together. They kept asking him questions and he told them that he has a woman he loves dearly, but it's not Luna or any of his ex girlfriends, and he'll be introducing her to the public soon, he told them to clear his path that he has something to attend to. The reporters cleared his path, and he entered his car, he rushed directly to Cathy's house, he knocked on her door and she opened it, she looked at him and turned away, then Chris pulled her back and hugged her. He said he was sorry, and didn't know Luna would do something like that, Chris said he'll make it up to her and would be announcing their relationship the next day in his press conference. Cathy looked at him and said there's no need, Chris replied that he has to, Cathy said she understands him and knows that having a celebrity boyfriend isn't easy if you don't have a great mentality and the patience, she added that she trusts him wholeheartedly. Chris was shocked upon hearing that, he held her hands and looked at her eyes, he said he's grateful for having someone like her in his life. Cathy said no one can come in between them as long as they love and understand each other. Chris replied yes, Cathy smiled at him, he said he's hungry and wants to eat street food, Cathy said he can't that it's not healthy and that she'll prepare some food for him. Chris said she can do that some other time, he asked her to get ready so they can go out to get something to eat, Cathy told him that she wants to change her clothes, Chris replied no that she looks beautiful, Cathy said that her dressing is a bit casual, Chris replied casual dressing looks good on her. Cathy agreed and they set out together, they drove across the road and stopped by at a noodles joint, Cathy looked at him and said Chris did you brought me out just to eat noodles outside, it's something I can prepare. Chris said he doesn't want to disturb her, and wants to enjoy the noodles with the love of his life, the taste will definitely be superb, Cathy drew his lips forward and said he's a glutton, Chris replied he's happy to be silly when he's with her, Cathy said he's shameless and he pecked her forehead. They got down from the car and ordered noodles, they were served immediately and Chris ate his bowl of noodles happily, Cathy smiled and said there's nothing she can do about him being silly. Chris raised his head and looked at Cathy with a serious look on his face, Cathy asked if he felt offended by her words, he answered no, he said that the last time he ate noodles there was when his parents were still alive, his countenance changed and he became sad, Cathy held his hands and said he shouldn't be too sad that she's there for him, and they'll have an happy home soon. Chris smiled and told Cathy thanks, she asked if the noodles joint had existed for a long time, he answered yes and used to visit there with his parents when he was little, his parents enjoyed the noodles. When they were done, and was about to leave, the owner came to meet him and asked how he's been, she said it's been a long time. Chris answered he's fine, the woman asked who Cathy is, he said she's his girlfriend, the woman said she's so pretty, she added that she sees his poster everywhere and is happy he's doing well, she packed some noodles for them, they thanked her and they left. On their way home, Chris stopped by a mall, Cathy asked him what he wanted to get, he said just a few things for her, Cathy said there's no need to, Chris said it's his responsibility to take care of her, she works overtime sometimes and doesn't eat much, so she needs something to replenish her body. Cathy said okay and they got down from the car, the went inside and bought some provision for her, on their way out, Mary bumped into Cathy, she was entering inside. Cathy greeted her and she responded well, Mary asked her what she's doing there and Cathy said she went to get some stuff together with her boyfriend Chris, she introduced him to Mary and they exchanged pleasantries. Mary was surprised to see that Cathy's boyfriend is so handsome and is a star, she thought Cathy was dating James. Cathy asked Mary how she's been and where she is working now, she replied she's working in a finance company and is doing well. Chris said it's getting late and they have to go to work tomorrow, so Cathy told Mary that she'll meet up with her after work tomorrow, Mary replied alright that she'd text her the address, and bid them goodnight. Cathy and Chris left and he dropped her at her house, Chris asked if he couldn't stay over, but Cathy said she wouldn't be able to sleep if he's around, so he wished her a good night and left.

CHAPTER 9

THE SOLUTION

Cathy was working in her office when she received a message from Mary, they were to meet by 07pm at a park nearby. She called Mary and told her she'd be seeing her. Cathy assigned some tasks to her team members while she reviewed some files. She continued the project she handed to Nancy and was thinking of a solution, the company could not lose the project as they had invested much money into it. She made some business calls and told the company they're working with Healthy Fruits, which deals mainly with fruits and fruit drinks, the company makes grape wine as well and MLT wanted to work with them as Healthy Farm would be celebrating their company anniversary.

Chris had a press conference that day, some reporters wanted to know the relationship between him and Luna, he was asked to clarify the matter. Chris replied that Luna is his ex girlfriend and there's nothing going on between them. A reporter asked why they're intimate in the pictures that was posted online. Chris said they only ate a meal together as friends, and he has a woman in his life already.

WE MEET AGAIN

The reporters were asking if he could show them the woman. Chris paused for a while, he remembered telling Cathy that he'd be announcing their relationship, but he wanted to do it in a good manner. Chris replied that she's a strong woman of a positive mindset and a loving heart, fate brought them together as they've had some encounters a long time ago. The reporters asked if he could tell them her name, Chris answered no and that he'd announce her to the world when the time comes. The reporters asked Chris how people are going to believe his word, he replied it doesn't matter if anyone believes or not and left. The reporters followed him and asked if he could tell them a few things more, but Chris said he cannot as he has other things to do.

Luna watched the press conference and called Chris, he picked and asked her what's up. Luna asked if he could show her the lady he was talking about, Chris replied no and told her he's hanging up. Luna said she only wanted to know the lady that won his heart over, and that she can't possibly be an ordinary person. Chris answered that his lover is not an ordinary person definitely, she's unique, he hung up after that. Luna called her manager and asked her to hire someone who will spy on Chris. Her manager told her there's no need to and should not try to find out some things, but Luna insisted. Her manager said it isn't part of her work to do such, Luna looked at her and held her hand, she said she wants to be happy so she needs to know about Chris movement, and it's only her manager that can help her to handle the task. Her manager agreed and hired someone to spy on Chris and report his movements.

Cathy came up with a solution on how to work with Healthy Fruits and was drafting a proposal when Chris call entered, she picked it and Chris told about the press conference he did and that he wasn't able to announce his woman. Cathy said it's okay and there was no way he could announce her at such moment and that they don't need anyone's permission to continue their love. Chris said her words are right, and asked when she'd done at work so he can pick her up. Cathy answered that she has plans with Mary by 07pm, Chris said ohh that he remember Mary asking to see her. Cathy asked him what he's thinking, and Chris replied he's always thinking about her, Cathy laughed and Chris asked her what's she's thinking, Cathy replied she's thinking of how MLT can work with Healthy Fruits for their company anniversary project. Chris said so he's not on her mind but work alone, Cathy answered that he's important to her but that is what is on her mind. Chris asked her whether Healthy Fruits CEO was Anderson, a middle aged man, Cathy replied yes and asked him how he got to know. Chris said he's his acquaintance and he did a performance for him on his birthday. Chris added that she should try coming up with a proposal on how to make Healthy Fruits grape wine a demand in the market. Cathy said that Healthy Fruits focus mainly on fruits, Chris replied that the company produces fruit, but their grape wines has not been a successful product in the market, despite the company producing high quality fruits. Cathy asked how she would go about it, Chris replied she should gather some information about the grape wine, and come up with a way for it to enter market. He added that Anderson's wife enjoyed the grape wines, but only fruits sold well, also Anderson started his company by producing wine, but after experiencing a major setback in his business, he started producing fruits and did well in it. He said the wine is one of his dreams and if MLT could make it come through, he'd be happy. He said Anderson knows how to make it, but doesn't know how to sell it, which leaves room for MLT's assistance, so the point is to make a proposal that can help him sell. Chris said Anderson would have seen a lot of proposals on how to improve his fruits business, but might have not seen one on his wine and doing that is helping him solve a problem. Cathy said that he's right and would work on it and thanked Chris for helping her out. Chris said there's no need to be thankful, helping her out is his responsibility, he said they'll talk later and ended the call. Cathy reviewed the documents Nancy sent to her again, she found out it only contained some information about Healthy Fruits fruit business and nothing about the grape wine. Cathy started to make some findings and didn't find out anything, she went to her colleagues office and asked her team members to find out any information they can about Healthy Fruits and its CEO, but they all found out nothing new. Cathy checked Anderson's LinkedIn profile and went through it thoroughly, he saw that Anderson had once posted his grape wines some years ago. She told her team members about Anderson's grape wines and they were surprised and said Anderson makes only fruits, she showed them his post on LinkedIn and they said oh no, it can't be, they said it's their first time hearing such. Cathy asked them to share their opinions on how Fresh Fruits grape wines can be sold in the market. They all shared their views while she listened to them. Cathy told them to send their data to her and left for her office, she drafted a proposal. She worked for a few hours and took a little break.

Cathy left her office around 06:30pm and headed for the

park, she walked there and got to the place by 06:55pm. Mary was already waiting, Cathy saw her where she sat and approached her, they exchanged greetings and she sat beside her. Mary asked about Chris, Cathy replied he's fine, Mary asked how their relationship is going, Cathy said they're doing well. Cathy asked if Mary is in touch with James and she said she's not, Cathy asked her if Mary intends going back to the relationship with James. Mary paused for a while and said she can't because of what has happened between them, and regarding the company's issue too. She added that James would feel uncomfortable being seen with MLT's traitor, Cathy held her hands and said she's not, she said she acted that way out of impulsiveness, though it was wrong of her to do that. Mary said she still have feelings for James though, and that when she acted that way, she thought there was something going on between her and James, but now it's not worth the fight. Cathy said she heard Mary gave up being an artist and followed the same career path as James. Mary replied she did so she could always support James, but giving up your future for someone isn't a good decision. Cathy said she could still be an artist, Mary replied yes that she still loves drawing, Cathy said she could open an art gallery then since she has the talents and money. Mary smiled and said she intends giving it a try too, Cathy said it's a brave decision and would feel happy with her work. Mary looked at Cathy and stared at her, Cathy asked her why kept looking at her, Mary answered that she's surprised she could meet up with her despite what happened between them. Cathy said all that happened is in the past already and Mary was the one who recommended her for promotion. Mary thanked her and said she enjoyed her company, she said it's getting late and they should leave now. She added that she'd take Cathy home, Cathy said there's no need, but Mary insisted since she drove there herself. Cathy agreed and Mary drove her home, when they got to her house, they saw Chris standing outside. Mary greeted Chris and bid them goodnight, Chris turned to Cathy and said her relationship with Mary has gotten better. Cathy said she's not petty to keep grudges with Mary and she enjoyed her company. Chris said it's good she thinks that way since there's nothing to gain from being against Mary, after all James who could have been the reason for their strife has nothing to do with Cathy. He asked Cathy how the project she's handling is, and she said she has gotten some leads and told him some updates.

CHAPTER 10

THE LEAK

Cathy was going through some documents at work when an announcement was passed along that there's a meeting scheduled by 2pm. It was 1:30pm, she quickly printed the drafted proposal, made some photocopies, and did some necessary things, after then she rushed to the conference room where they held the meeting. They were discussing on taking acquisition of smaller companies, some of the shareholders agreed, while others did not. The CEO, Bryan said the acquisition can wait, and asked for update about the Fresh Fruits project. Cathy stood up and shared the photocopies of the project, only a few shareholders and staff were present. One of the directors asked her what she meant by promoting Fresh Fruits grape wines, Cathy replied and stated her reasons. She said other companies would be focusing on the company's fruits, and she thinks it's better to focus on a different aspect, also Fresh Fruits started by making grape wines. They went through the proposal and agreed with her, then the meeting ended. Anderson's secretary, Myles called Cathy and said his boss had asked to see her the following day regarding the project, he told her the time and hung up. Those that attended the meeting missed their lunch break, but went to the company's canteen during their free time. Cathy went as well and ordered her meal, James approached her and sat opposite her. She asked him if he planned to eat there before or came because of her, he said it's exactly because of that, to see her. Cathy asked him if he had anything to say and James replied yes, he asked if she met with Mary, Cathy replied yes. James said she shouldn't have because of what happened to her in the company. Cathy said Mary acted that way due to some reasons and it doesn't matter if anyone is meeting with her. She asked James that isn't Mary his childhood friend, and he replied yes. Cathy said he should show her his support then since Mary would be opening an art gallery soon. James was a bit surprised and said he'll meet with her during weekend, he asked Cathy about Chris and she replied he's doing well. James said she's lucky to meet such a great guy, Cathy replied there's someone who cherishes him as well and is willing to do anything for him. James said what happened between him and Mary is in the past and has no intention of going back to the relationship, and now he only has Cathy in his mind. Cathy replied it can't work out between them as she belongs to another person, she left and headed for her office.

WE MEET AGAIN

Chris picked up Cathy from the office during evening, she looked quite upset and he asked her what's wrong. Cathy replied she wondered how James could act that way, Mary was the woman he once claimed to love and how can he avoid her in such situation and even cut off their ties. Chris replied that some men are that way, you only see them when things are going well and then they leave you when you are going through circumstances. He told Cathy not to think about such and be happy, Cathy replied alright and smiled. Chris didn't take her home and brought her to a bar instead, Cathy was surprised and asked why they're there. Chris asked her if she didn't like to drink, he said he remember she once drank with James, and why can't she drink with him also. He asked If she liked James instead and not him, Cathy pinched him and said it's not so. Chris asked that it's what then, Cathy replied she's not in the mood to drink, Chris said a glass isn't bad, but since she doesn't want to, they can leave then. Cathy said she'll take a drink then, Chris said no, that she doesn't have to and he would never force her to do something against her will. Chris held her hands and told her not to worry about anything, a college student happened to be there and took their pictures. Chris and Cathy weren't aware, Cathy said she suddenly feel like drinking, Chris said she's so indecisive, Cathy replied whatever. They left after taking a few drinks, Chris dropped her at her house and bid her a goodnight. The student posted the pictures online the following day and some reporters saw it and wrote articles. Some used the headline "singer Chris secret lover revealed", some wrote "singer Chris relationship exposed", the reporters used various headlines, Chris saw the articles online but ignored it. Chris had a show that day, some reporters had already been waiting for him there, as he got down, they surrounded him and asked him to give comments on the pictures posted online, they asked if it's true, and if that was the lady he once mentioned. Chris replied that the lady is indeed his lover but he has nothing else to say and does not want to be late for his show, the reporters asked him to tell them about the lady, he said he will at his convenient time and hope they won't be bothering him, he asked them to clear his way as he has to perform, they did and he went inside.

Cathy visited Fresh Fruits regarding the project, on getting there, she called the CEO, Anderson's secretary that she's in the company, and the secretary told her that she'll come to meet her right away. The secretary came and took her to the CEO's office. Cathy had made appointment earlier under MLT's name, Cathy and Anderson exchanged greetings, and she took her sit. Anderson was a middle aged man with a warm heart, he asked her why she came, Cathy replied that it's because of the company's upcoming anniversary and hopes MLT can take up the task. Anderson asked why, Cathy replied it's because she's confident in MLT, she handed the proposal to him and asked him to go through it. Anderson said there's so many companies wanting the offer and he already intends to give it to another company. Cathy said MLT is focusing on marketing Fresh Fruits grape wines giving it a fresh and different start, Anderson was surprised and looked at her, he said it might not sell well in the market. Cathy replied that if he doesn't try, he won't know whether it will sell or not, Anderson said he'll go through it and contact her. He asked her how she knew about the grape wines, she said she happened to see it under his posts on LinkedIn and thinks is a great idea, Anderson said he's touched and that his wife had always loved them, he said he has a meeting soon that Cathy should take her leave. Cathy bid him goodbye and left for MLT, she boarded a taxi and got off in front of the company's building. She entered the company and was heading for her office. Some of the staff had seen the pictures of Cathy and Chris holding hands which was posted online and watched the news where Chris said she's indeed his lover Some staff were staring at her, and was gossiping about her. Some said she approached the man because of his fame and money, and such relationship won't last, some said Chris cares about her indeed and they've been together for quite some time, some said she can't endure seeing ladies hover around him, everyone was stating their views. Cathy overheard them and greeted them, they asked her why she came late to work, she said she went somewhere because of the project she was handling, a staff said Cathy is really diligent in her work and is an ace in the company, it's no surprise she has a celebrity boyfriend. Cathy smiled and said she has work to do and took her leave, they were surprised at her reaction, they thought she'd argue with them or something and went to their offices. Cathy entered her office and was going through her computer when a call entered through the office telephone, it was Ann, the CEO's secretary, the CEO had requested to see her. She closed the files, locked her computer and headed for the CEO's office, on getting there, the CEO was turning his back while looking at the window. She greeted him and he asked her to take her sit, she was wondering what's going on, the CEO turned to her and asked her why she isn't sitting. Cathy replied it's nothing, the CEO smiled and sat down, Cathy took her sit as well. The CEO, Bryan, asked her if she knows why he asked to see her, she replied no and thinks maybe it's because of the Fresh

WE MEET AGAIN

Fruits project, Bryan said it's part of the reason, but it's not exactly why. Cathy asked if she can know the reason, Bryan asked her if she watch news at all, she replied that she does once in a while, Bryan said it'll be helpful for her work, he reached for his phone and showed her the video of Chris being interrogated by reporters. Bryan said she knows she's in a relationship, and the company isn't against such, and she admires the fact that she kept such a low profile. He added that he thought she and James would make a great match, but her boyfriend seems sincere as well, he wished them luck. Cathy was surprised and didn't know what to say, she thanked the CEO, Bryan told her to make sure she handles the project well and not focus too much on the relationship, Cathy replied she won't disappoint him, she asked if she could tell him about the project updates, but the CEO replied that she shouldn't yet and just put in more effort into it. He told her she can take her leave now, and Cathy left for her office.

CHAPTER 11

YOU ARE SWEET

At MLT, Cathy was interviewing some interns when a call came in, it was from Joyce, Anderson's secretary who relayed information that Anderson has chosen MLT to handle the project. Cathy finished her interview with the interns, then she recruited two to her department. She sent a message to the company's confidential group on Whatsapp which consisted of her, the CEO, James, and two other people and informed them of the project. The CEO called her and told her to handle it well and not let down the company's trust, Cathy assured him of it. She was sorting out some files regarding the project when James entered her office. She was so carried away by what she was doing that she didn't notice James standing in front of her, James knocked the desk, then she looked up. Cathy asked him what he was doing in her office, he replied he came to check on how the project is going. She said she's just sorting out some files on it, James asked her when she started that she's done so quick. Cathy replied she already worked on it beforehand and is doing some documentations. James complimented her and told her to do it well, Cathy replied thanks and continued with her work.

WE MEET AGAIN

Chris was driving along a pathway when he noticed a car following him from behind. He called Cathy and told her he'd be at her workplace soon to congratulate her on getting the project. Cathy told him to drive safely and said she'd be expecting him. Chris made some turns and noticed that the car was still following him, it was a quiet place with few cars passing along. Chris felt upset and wanted to know the person trailing him, he made some turns and wanted to double cross the car when his car brakes lost control and he hit a signpost with force, he wasn't using his safety belt which caused him to hit his head against his windscreen. He was bleeding but he got out of the car nonetheless, he approached the person trailing him and to his surprise it was his friend, Arnold who just got back from France, he went to pursue his career as a chef. Chris was pissed, Arnold apologized and told him to go to the hospital in his car, and he'd get Chris car fixed. Chris said he didn't leave aside his silly attitude of scaring people, Arnold asked him where he's going to, Chris said uhm and couldn't remember, Arnold waved his hands in front of him, Chris rushed to his car to get his phone. He saw the calls he's missed from Cathy and her message too, but couldn't remember her. Cathy called again, Chris picked it, she asked him what's going on with him in a worried tone, she asked if he's not coming again, which made Chris remember he had to see someone, he told Cathy he had an accident and intends on going to the hospital since he couldn't remember some things. He said he can't recall who Cathy is but feels she's someone he's close to. Cathy asked him to drop the hospital address when he gets there and he said he will, and ended the call. Arnold asked Chris who he was talking to on the phone, Chris replied it's a lady, he doesn't remember much about her, but he feels she's someone special to him. He called his manager and told him he had an accident and his car is damaged, he told him his location and said he's heading to the hospital in his friend's car. His manager asked him how come his friend is there, he replied he'd explain all that later, his manager replied he'd handle it and would check on him.

Chris was admitted in a nearby hospital, he sent the address to Cathy and his manager, he was first treated. The doctor had him take some X-rays to know what part of his head is injured, he was allocated a ward, the doctor came to see him after then, asked him how he's feeling. Chris said he feels hurt due to the accident, but he feels somewhat nervous as well. He said there's someone he can't remember but he feels she's someone dear to him.

WE MEET AGAIN

The doctor said not to worry much, with frequent contact with the person, he'd remember her with time, he asked Chris to rest on time and then took his leave. Arnold was with him through the whole process, he told Chris to get some rest and that he wants to attend to some things. Not long after, Cathy arrived at the hospital, she asked for his ward, she was directed there, it was a VIP ward. She came in and saw Chris lying down with his head bandaged, she sat beside him, held his hand with tears in her eyes. Chris asked who she is, she said she's Cathy, his girlfriend and closest friend. Chris was trying hard to remember, but Cathy told him to take it easy and not force himself, she bought fruits and food for him and asked him to eat. Chris was staring at her in the eyes, she urged him to eat, on opening the food, it was Chris favourite meal, he thanked her and started eating. Cathy smiled at him and asked if he wanted her to feed him, he replied yes, Cathy laughed and did. Chris told her he's surprised how he could open up to her despite the fact that he doesn't remember her, but he feels relaxed with her. Cathy looked at him and said if he doesn't remember their memories, they can create new ones. Cathy's phone rang, it was from the office, she left without taking a leave permission, Cathy replied the person over the phone that she'd be in the office soon. She told Chris that she had to leave as she has things to attend to, Chris said it's alright, Cathy said she'd check on him in the night and bid him goodbye. On her way out, she met Arnold at the reception. He greeted her and she smiled while walking confidently.

Arnold got to Chris ward and met him smiling, he looked at him with bewilderment and asked if he was okay, Chris replied he is. Arnold looked at his table and saw fruits, water and a flask, he asked Chris where he got it from, he replied it's from Cathy. Arnold was trying to get the statement, he asked who Cathy is, Chris frowned and told Arnold to stop questioning him. Chris said Cathy got the fruits, water and food for him, it was the lady that called him then and she just left not quite long. Arnold asked if it was the special girl, Chris replied yes, he added that he wants to remember her as soon as possible, she's so loving, caring and understanding. Arnold said it'd have been lovely to meet her, Chris said yeah and it would be more lovely to recover his memories of her too. Arnold smiled and asked Chris to make a guess, Chris seem shocked a bit, and said he doesn't know how to make guesses and he isn't in the mood after making him end up this way. Arnold told Chris that he has tended his apology earlier, Chris replied it's not enough, he asked Arnold about the new girl he's crushing on. Arnold was like wow, how did you know I have a new crush! Chris said he guessed that's what the situation is, he asks him to guess when he meets someone new. Arnold said well, I met a beautiful lady at the reception today and her smile is so lovely, she was putting on a blue shirt with pants. Chris said that's my girlfriend Cathy, Arnold said how're you sure she's your girlfriend, do you have a picture of her? Chris said oh that's true, I should have. He opened his phone, went through his pictures and saw images of him and Cathy, anyone could tell they were in love, Cathy's picture was his Whatsapp wallpaper too. Chris got carried away by looking at Cathy's picture, Arnold said so that's his sister-in-law, you have a great taste, Chris, it's just a bit saddening that you don't remember her. Chris looked at him and said he'll recover his memories of her soon at this rate.

Cathy got back to the office, the CEO asked her to see him, she rushed to his office, knocked on the door, and was told to come in. The CEO, Bryan asked her why she left without notice as an important figure in the company. She replied something urgent came up, Bryan asked what it was, she didn't want to reply, Bryan said he's not trying to pry into her personal life but he's curious what could be more important than work to Cathy, could it be Chris... Cathy looked at him with a sad look on her face, Bryan said she could open up to him, Cathy replied Chris had an accident, got injured in the head and lost only his memories of her, so she had to rush over to the hospital to check on him. She added that she apologize for not taking a leave, Bryan asked how he's doing now, Cathy replied he's fine and would recover soon, Bryan asked if he could check on him, Cathy answered yes and thanked him. Bryan said now that Chris is fine, she should put her mind at rest, and how is the project going. She replied she's done with the project and it remains the execution, Bryan smiled and said he knew Cathy would never disappoint the company, Cathy thanked him and took her leave.

CHAPTER 12

WE CARE ABOUT YOU

At the hospital,

Chris was lying on the hospital bed when a call came in, it was Cathy. She asked how he's doing now and he replied he's getting better, and the only thing he's yet to recover is his memories. Cathy replied he's gonna recover it soon and shouldn't force it, Chris said alright he's gonna be patient then. Cathy asked if he's cool with her boss visiting him, that he wants to check on him. Chris answered he's very much okay with it, Cathy asked again whether he has eaten, he answered yes that Arnold brought some food earlier. Cathy said it's good then and that she'd visit him during noon with her boss. Chris asked Cathy whether she's doing fine, she replied yes that she's doing fine, he asked her how her work is going, she replied work Is fine and everything is under control. He asked further if she didn't get into trouble at work because of him, she replied no, that the issue was sorted out. Chris paused a bit on the phone, Cathy asked what's wrong, he said he's sorry for not keeping her in the deepest place of his heart, Cathy replied he shouldn't talk that way. Chris replied if he really had kept her there, he wouldn't have lost his memories of her, Cathy answered he shouldn't feel sad or blame himself and that everything has a reason. Chris said you remain my adviser and confidante Cathy, I'll always remember you from now on, Cathy replied he should get some rest and they'll talk more when they see, Chris told her to take care of herself, she replied thanks and you too, and hanged up.

Cathy called her team members for a brief meeting, she asked them how the work she assigned to them is going, and they narrated their updates to her. She also educated them on different techniques they can use as a financial analyst, she talked about some common problems in their field and how they can solve it. They asked her about how projects gets assigned to her and how she handles it on time. She answered, understand the market and economy, know your competitors and pose solutions in a different way, you should also study the person you intend to work with and earn his/her trust. You can only do a great job if you and your client are on the same page, cooperation matters. Also, when projects gets assigned to you, handle it on time, if you have any questions or issues, you can come to me. Her team members thanked her, Cathy waved her hand and said they're team members, it's only right for her to do that. Her burden would be lessened, when they're all doing well at their end. She added that she would try to fix a date to educate them on some survival skills, and dismissed them.

Jack, one of the interns that was assigned to Cathy's team was watching the news on his phone, so Kate a new employee who's also in Cathy's team asked him to get down to work and stop pressing his phone. Jack replied it's none of her business, Cathy said they should be conversant with the economy and he's only trying to do that by watching news. Kate replied it's not every news you should watch, filter out some and focus mainly on what's in your line of interest and field. Jack looked at her and nodded his head, Kate asked him what's up, he didn't reply and continued watching the news, Kate was about to take her leave when Jack held her hand. Kate was surprised and removed her hand from his grip, Jack said come and see Kate, he drew her closer and they watched the news together. The rest of the team members were curious of what's happening and went to check what they were watching. One of them asked, "is it because Cathy has returned to her office, that's why you act in an unruly manner?" Another said, "leave them, they're new here, but they shouldn't cause disruption with our work." Another person said "what do they know, they're obviously in love and even display it at work by watching news together, I get sick seeing this sight." Jack asked them to calm down and not make wild guesses and that the news is about Chris, they all exclaimed Chris!! Kate said yeah, it's about the singer Chris, he had an accident yesterday. "But why wasn't it announced?" one of them asked. Jack replied he doesn't know, maybe Chris agency didn't want the news to be leaked, but he got hurt and was admitted in the hospital. "But there was CCTV at the site, why didn't they check the video footage in time, how would Cathy feel when she hears this, she's so burdened with work" one of them exclaims. "She'll be fine" another answered, Cathy is a strong woman. Kate asked, "should we tell Cathy about this? she really need to know about it". As they were deliberating on whether to let Cathy know or not, she came in, she was holding some files in her hand.

They were astonished on seeing her. They quickly went back to their desks, Cathy was looking confused and could not figure out what's going on. "I remember the last time I saw this kind of scenery, it was about Chris, there was some news and rumors" said Cathy. Her team members looked at each other and muttered. "Cathy why're you here? You could have just called us to help you in bringing these files, you don't have to stress yourself with these little tasks" Louis said. Cathy replied I dropped a message on the group, but didn't get any reply, I didn't wanna bother anyone with calls, that's why I'm here, so what's going on. One of the team members, Anita whispered to Kate to tell her, Kate told Anita to say it her herself. Jack took a deep breath and said Chris had an accident yesterday, he has been admitted in the hospital, I saw it on the news, and we know the affection you have for him, please stay strong for us all, we really care about you, don't be too sad. The rest of the team members nodded their heads in agreement and urged Cathy to be strong, they told her he'll be fine and they wished him a quick recovery. Cathy looked at them and paused for a while, she said she knew about it already, and has gone to see him yesterday. She thanked them and added that he's in a good condition, Louis said "I know Cathy would always be strong, Kate said "I admire you Cathy, you remain yourself even in situations like this." Cathy handed the files to Jack, she told them she already explained they're gonna do on the group, and she took her leave. The team members stared at her in admiration and respect, they said among themselves "so she knew about it already and still remained in good shape". Anita said she's her role model, Louis urged them to get back to their work.

Cathy was already in her office when her phone rang, it

was Bryan, she picked it and he asked her whether she's free so they can go to visit Chris. She answered she's free, and has no urgent tasks in hand, Bryan replied good! that she should meet him at the reception, and ended the call. Cathy rushed out of her office and went to the reception, Bryan was already there, she greeted him and they set out together. The company staff looked at Cathy and wondered what's going on, they said to themselves, Cathy is out for a new project, she's indeed the ace in our company. One of them said, who knows what she's up to, maybe she's trying to cling onto the CEO now that Chris had accident. "Accident!! but why didn't we hear about it", some of them asked. The staff who told them about the accident replied that the news just got leaked, Cathy didn't even go to see her boyfriend, she's obviously trying to seduce the CEO. One of the staff answered, "Cathy is not that type of person, she's must be out for a new task" and dismissed them.

Bryan stopped by a convenient store along the way and bought some fruits for Chris, while Cathy bought some snacks, he asked her whether Chris would like them, Cathy replied he would, Bryan said alright, that they should get going then. They went back to the car, Cathy asked Bryan why they didn't set off with his driver, he replied he just felt like driving today and he thinks Chris might feel uncomfortable if they're many. Cathy smiled and said, there's no need to be too cautious around Chris, he's a cool guy, Bryan asked, really? Cathy said yeah and three is not a multitude, he's a lively type. Bryan said well, you know the way celebrities are, we try to please them, and I'm a fan of Chris, so I should be cautious.

They got to the hospital, and went to the ward where Chris is, they knocked on the door, the nurse on duty opened it, he was writing some lyrics and looked up to see who entered. "Chris", Cathy called him, he approached her and hugged her, Bryan greeted him, and Chris extended an handshake to him. "So this is my boss, he's been more like a brother to me", Cathy said. Chris was surprised and thanked him for looking after Cathy, Bryan smiled and said it's nothing, looking after the employees is part of a CEO's duty, also Cathy is a very important figure in the company. He handed the fruits to Chris, he was surprised and happy, he said I didn't know you got this for me, I'm really moved, Cathy's got a good boss. He looked at Cathy and asked if she won't introduce him to her boss also, Cathy replied she's sorry that it skipped her mind, but he doesn't really need introduction, who doesn't know Chris Love. "But that's not what I wanna hear Cathy, introduce me rightly",

Chris said. Cathy held Chris hand and said to Bryan, meet my lover Chris, the one who's got all my heart. Chris smiled and said that's what I wanna hear; "I guess I should get going now and not disrupt your mood", Bryan said. "Thank you so much for the love, I'm still gonna meet with you for a proper introduction", Chris replied. The doctor came in as they were talking and said Chris can get discharged today, Arnold happened to walk in at the moment, he waved at Cathy then left with the nurse on duty and helped with the discharge procedure, while Bryan took his leave.

Cathy helped Chris to pack, Chris looked at her and said there's no need to rush, she replied they can set off when Arnold is done and resting at home would be better. Chris said alright, and asked her what's her plan for tomorrow. She replied it's weekend and would love to visit her sister, she paused for a while and looked at Chris in the eyes. He asked her what's wrong, she replied, do you know the news reported your accident, he answered yes he's aware of it, his manager informed him. Cathy said it's gonna be fine, Chris asked her why she said so, she replied she didn't really know what to say; by the way, I haven't been able to meet Arnold properly. Chris replied I'll let you guys meet each other and talk well, we can do that when we're home. Arnold came in, and exchanged pleasantries with Cathy. "I'm sorry I didn't greet you properly when I entered earlier" Arnold said. Cathy replied it's alright, tending to Chris is more important, thank you for taking care of him for me. Arnold laughed and said there's no need to be thankful, his facial expression changed and he looked a bit sad. Cathy asked him what's wrong, he answered he caused Chris to be in such state, so he has to make up for it. Chris went near and pat him on the shoulder, he told him not to feel sad about it, he's doing fine now. "Let's head for home", Chris added, Arnold took Chris bag, while Chris held Cathy and they went out of the hospital. Chris called his manager and told him he's been discharged, and is on his way home, his manager said he should be careful and ensure he rest well, Chris told him not to worry, Cathy would take care of him and ended the call. He entered Arnold's car and sat at the back with Cathy, while Arnold drove, Cathy handed the snacks to him. Chris held her hand and said so you got me something, Cathy replied she didn't know what to buy and doesn't wanna buy fruits, her boss already bought that, and she can't bring him some food since Arnold brought some earlier, so she thought snacks was the best option. Chris smiled and said "you're so considerate, I'm happy to have you by my side". Arnold shouted "I'm happy to have you as my sister in law", how about you meet with her sister tomorrow Chris? he added. Chris replied that's a good idea, he turned to Cathy and said we'll visit your sister together, Cathy answered it's alright, my sister would welcome you since you're a dedicated guy and didn't mistreat me.

CHAPTER 13

MY PASSION

Arnold helped Chris to drop his bag in his room when they got home and started rushing out. Chris stared at him in a confused manner and looked at Cathy, he asked Arnold what's up, and where he's heading to. Arnold replied he's got an appointment with someone and is late already. "Did you forget you're meeting someone?", asked Cathy. "Yeah, I did, I just suddenly remembered I have to meet with a client", said Arnold. "I thought you were probably going to meet with a friend or someone, you should be on your way then," said Cathy. Arnold replied, "thanks Cathy, take care of Chris", and left. Cathy moved closer to Chris and asked why he didn't say anything to Arnold apart from the question he asked him earlier. Chris replied he didn't know what to say as Arnold was in a rush. "Ohh that's the case, I thought you became a quiet person already", said Cathy. "I'm still the same person, besides not saying anything doesn't mean I'm quiet, there's still a lot to discuss with him", replied Chris. "Anyway, let's put Arnold aside and discuss about us." Chris added. "So who should we start with?", Cathy asked. Chris held her hand, and asked her to sit, while he sat beside her, he looked at her eyes and said "let's start with you Cathy, when do you intend for us get married." Cathy asked, "can I be honest with you", Chris replied, "you can, I'd really love it if you can". Cathy said, "as soon as you're ready, I always am, it has always been my wish to get married to you, we've been dating for some while now and we have connections with each other". Chris said, "I love you Cathy, and I love the way I feel when I'm with you, you complete me", he ran short of words then kissed her, he began to recover his memories while kissing her and continued with the kiss. He stopped and looked at her, Cathy asked him what's with the look, he answered he remembers it all now, how they met and everything, and hugged her. Cathy wrapped her hands around him in return and said it's good he's recovered his memories. Chris whispered to Cathy and asked if she'd love to stay for the night, she replied she'll consider it. "Don't forget we're going to my sister's place tomorrow", she added. "I won't, we're definitely going to see her", Chris replied.

Arnold went to Classic gallery and stayed outside, the person he kept an appointment with was the owner and they've never met, he called her and told her he's outside. The person told him to come in and that someone is waiting at the reception to bring him to her office. Arnold went in, met the receptionist and told him about his appointment, the receptionist asked if he was Mr Arnold, he answered yes. The receptionist asked the lady beside him to take Arnold to their boss office, "you can follow her, Mr Arnold", he said. Arnold followed the lady, he looked at the structure of the gallery and admired it. They got to the boss office, the lady knocked, a voice asked them to come in, and they did. "Mr Arnold is here", said the lady; "you can leave now", the boss replied. The lady took her leave, the boss was a lady in white shirt with pink pants, she stood facing the window, Arnold was curious to know who she was. She turned and greeted Arnold with a smile, Arnold was astonished by her beauty and said he didn't expect the boss to be a beautiful young lady. "Oh you flatter me Mr Arnold, you're a good looking young man, you can have your sit" said the boss. Arnold laughed, sat down, and said, "I guess I have a lot to learn from you when it comes to speaking softly". Cathy sat and said, "I'm sorry for giving you a proper introduction, I'm Mary Cobbs, CEO of classic gallery, you can call me Mary". "You have a nice name, your gallery is in order too, though I've only seen it online, but I love the structure. I'm sorry for coming later than the expected time, you can call me Arnold too, let's leave the formalities", said Arnold. "It's alright, I actually booked an appointment with you because I wanted you to work with me on my arts exhibition that's gonna hold soon. I'd love to use one of your meals for an artwork and I'd want you to make the meal too, so we can have a drawing of the meal, and the meal itself", said Mary. "I don't really get you, do you mean I should make a meal ready, and you're gonna make a drawing of the meal too, you wanna add it to your exhibition peace", asked Arnold. "Yeah, that's what I'm trying to say, I intend to do something different this time, so what meal do you think we can use", said Mary. "Well, we'd talk about this further, you should also familiarize yourself with the meal, the taste, look, and everything, it's gonna make it great, a food piece is also something nice", said Arnold. Mary replied, "I'd be hoping to hear from you, thanks for coming, I shouldn't take much of your time." "I'll give you a call to know when next we can meet, and probably discuss about some other things, can I take a look at the gallery", said Arnold. Mary replied he can, and told him to follow her, they went to the gallery, Arnold admired each piece and asked questions about it. "Mary I heard you were a financial analyst for long, and became an artist some months ago, how come your gallery looks like that of an artist that has been drawing for long", asked Arnold. "Drawing has always been my passion, I didn't do well as a financial analyst, so I decided to go back to where I belong, since I'm doing what makes me happy now, the gallery has been doing well", replied Mary. "Wow, you're so driven, I love your passion, we're similar in some ways. I didn't do well in college, I had wanted to become an engineer, a mechanical engineer to be precise, I loved motorbikes, and wished to make them; but I didn't do well in the areas that would make me become who I want. I started dealing in motorbikes, I invested my money in bikes and sold them, but I ended up in bankruptcy, so I decided to follow my passion which is cooking, traveled to France to become a certified chef, I'm doing well now, I run an hotel around here and I organize trainings too" said Arnold. Mary looked at him and said, "we met for a reason, and we both found happiness in our passion, which means no matter how long you've travelled in the wrong direction, you can always turn around". Arnold replied, "I'm happy that I knew you, finally met someone who understands me, I hope I can get to know you more". Mary replied, "we're friends now and business partners", and extended an handshake to him. "I'll like to be on my way soon, we'll discuss more on the phone", said Arnold. Mary replied, "you can get going then, I look forward to meeting you next time". Arnold nodded and took his leave, while Mary returned to her office.

It was the next day at Chris house, Cathy was still asleep on the bed when Chris got up beside her and prepared breakfast. She woke up an hour later, and didn't find Chris beside her, she wondered where he was and went to the sitting room to check if he was there. He wasn't there, she checked around the house and couldn't find him, so she went back to the room and saw him dressing up. "Chris where have you been, I've looked around for you, but didn't find you", asked Cathy. Chris replied, "I was in the bathroom, did you check there too, I'm sorry for making you worried". "Ohh I checked it, but you weren't there, I thought you went out, it's obvious you're just coming out of the shower, your hair is still wet", Cathy replied. "I'm here now Cathy, you should take your bathe too" said Chris. He handed a paper bag to her and said, "change into these clothes when you're done", he added. Cathy opened the bag and saw a beautiful short gown with matching flat shoes. "When did you get this Chris, how did you know my size too", Cathy asked. "I'm dating you baby, it's normal to know these things, I'm not telling you how I got to know though. You always wear pants, shirts and heels, you should wear something different this time, you should shower and get dressed, you know we're still going out", Chris answered. Cathy looked at him with surprise and hugged him; she said, "thanks for your care, I'll do as you say". Chris pecked her and said, "I'll be in the sitting room so you don't have to start looking for me again". "I nearly forgot, I got you a bathrobe", Chris added. He went to his closet and brought out another paper bag, he handed it to her. "Your skincare is in there too", Chris said. "You've virtually got everything ready Chris, I'm touched, I don't know how to express my gratitude" Cathy said. Chris replied, "show me your gratitude by staying with me, everything is ready, what's left is for you to move in". Cathy said, "I'll do that once we get married, we can't live apart from each other". Cathy changed into the bathrobe and went to the bathroom, while Chris went to the sitting room. Chris was playing a song on his guitar when Cathy was done and came to meet him, she was dressed up already. Chris admired her and said he loved her look, he took some pictures with her and posted it. He used the caption, "seeing her while practicing gives me happiness and inspiration, I can't wait to make her bear my name". Comments was flowing in: some said, "isn't that Cathy, she looks different and beautiful", "she's really lucky, she got Chris dedicated", "Cathy's finally taken my crush away", "you two should get married soon, you're a lovely couple", "seeing a beautiful woman like her everyday is indeed a blessing". Chris smiled while checking those comments, he held Cathy's hand and said they should eat now. "You posted those pics Chris, let me see it", said Cathy. Chris showed her his phone, Cathy scrolled through it and said, "you're already making it obvious that we're getting married, I haven't even gotten a ring yet". "Is ring the assurance of our relationship", asked Chris. "No, our love is the assurance, I'm hungry now", Cathy answered. "I wonder how it would feel getting it", she added. "Chris, we haven't prepared any meal yet and you're asking us to eat, I nearly thought there was food ready, or are you ordering something", Cathy asked. "I prepared food for us already while you were still asleep, you said you're hungry, we should eat now", Chris answered. Cathy hugged him and said, "you're such a darling". "When did you develop the attitude of hugging someone constantly", Chris asked. Cathy replied, "don't you like it, I can stop it if you don't." "I actually like you that way, don't ever change", Chris said. They went to the dinning room, and sat down, the food was dished in the flask, while some dishes were covered, there was fruits and water on the table too. Cathy opened a dish and something sparkled in her eyes, it was a ring, there was a letter in it too. Chris took out the ring and wore it on her finger, Cathy looked at him with surprise, and said "I didn't know you got all this ready, I'm so impressed." She read the letter, it says, "meeting you was predestined, you complete me, you're my passion, please become mine". Chris looked at Cathy's eyes and said, "I want you to become my family, let's get married", Cathy replied, "I will,

WE MEET AGAIN

I'll become not only your family, I'll also love you wholeheartedly just as you love me". Chris smiled, Cathy served the food, they ate, and headed for sister's place.

Cathy told Chris his sister's address, the got there and knocked the door. Her sister's husband, Williams came out, he was surprised to see Cathy and Chris and welcomed them. They went in, Williams continued staring at Chris, Cathy's sister, Phoebe came out of her room carrying her daughter, she was surprised to see Cathy, she hugged her and greeted Chris. "I know you're a busy woman, I'm happy you're here today, and who's the handsome man beside you", Phoebe asked, turning to Cathy. "I came to check on you, also to check on how my little princess is doing, she's all grown now", Cathy replied. Williams asked, "so I'm the only one you didn't come to see". Cathy replied, "I'm here to see you as well, also to introduce my boyfriend, Chris, he said he wants to meet you". Williams and Phoebe looked at each other, "but when did Cathy have a boyfriend", Phoebe asked. "I and Cathy have been together for quite some time, I hope you can give me the permission to be with her, I'm really in love with her and want to make her mine fully", Chris said. "You can be with her, I and my wife give you the permission, but you should remember not to hurt her feelings, or mistreat her, she's my family member", Williams said. "You look familiar, what do you do", Williams asked. "I'm an artiste", Chris replied. "Ohh you're the singer, Chris", you look more handsome in reality, Cathy brought home a cool guy", said Phoebe. "He's indeed that artiste, I love his songs, rumors says he's a cool man and a loyal guy, anyway take proper care of Cathy" Williams said. Cathy smiled and said, "Chris has been treating me so well, and I'm happy to have him, you know being a celebrity's girlfriend isn't easy, but I'm rest assured he's all mine". Chris said, "you gave me your heart and trust Cathy, it's my duty to take care of it". Cathy went near Phoebe and carried her daughter, she said, "babies grow so fast, she was still so little the last time I saw her". "Babies are lovely too, we should have ours soon so your niece can have someone to play with." Cathy looked at him and hit him, and said, "giving birth to a child is not easy, if you want a baby, just say it, don't use my niece as an excuse". "Alright, I actually want a baby too", Chris said. "Then you should get married soon", Phoebe said to Chris. "Yeah, I want both Cathy and a baby, but Cathy's my priority" Chris said. Phoebe's baby drew the ring in Cathy's hand, Cathy removed her hand, while Chris carried her. "What ring is that Cathy, I just saw it when my baby drew it", Phoebe asked. "It's my proposal ring, Chris gave it to me", Cathy answered. "Wow that's cool, ensure you continue in your love, understand, and tolerate each other", phoebe said. Williams asked if Chris is interested in playing chess, and he said yes, so they went outside and played it. Cathy remained inside with Phoebe and they catch up with some discussions. Williams asked Chris of his plans, and Chris told him his feelings for Cathy is real, they once met while they were younger and fate brought them together again, so he's not going to let her go. Williams said he wishes him the best and should bear in mind that being in love requires dedication and continuous efforts. Phoebe asked Cathy if she truly loves Chris, she replied yeah, she once met him some years ago, surprisingly, they met again, he's been good to her and had gotten her heart. She added that she doesn't wanna lose a great guy like him. Phoebe said it's good she loves him, but she should make sure she tries to retain her love and not listen to gossips, and trust the man she's with.

CHAPTER 14

SWEET MOMENTS

Chris left with Cathy during evening and dropped Cathy at her place. He made some enquires on how to register his marriage with Cathy and was told to come on Monday, with her. He called Cathy and told her about it, "so we're registering our marriage on Monday, I'll notify my sister so we can take photos together when we're done", Cathy said. "I'll notify Arnold, I thought of registering our marriage soon before having a main wedding later on." "That's good, I'm surprised it would be this fast, do you intend on disclosing it?", Cathy asked. "No I'm keeping it private, and if it gets out, it's not a bad thing either, I just don't feel like getting the media involved in my private affairs. Let's have dinner tomorrow, with Arnold", Chris said. "Alright dear, see you tomorrow", Cathy answered and hanged up. Cathy called her sister and told her about her marriage plans. "It's nice you'll be getting married to him soon, that way you can have him to yourself", Phoebe said. "Yeah, I was surprised when he told me about it and was happy too. I have work to do now, we'll talk later", Cathy answered. "So you called me just to tell me this, I'll inform Williams, we'll come together", Phoebe said. "I called you directly after speaking with Chris, take care of yourself, I love you sis, bye", Cathy replied and hanged up.

Arnold paid a visit to Chris house, he was sleeping on the couch, he was rehearsing before he got tired and slept off. Arnold knocked on the door for quite some time, but didn't get a reply, he called Chris too, but he was in a deep sleep and didn't hear his phone ringing. Arnold was wondering what could be going on, and decided to open the door, he knew Chris password and was able to enter inside. He saw Chris sleeping and tapped him, he woke up and was a bit surprised. "What're you doing here?", Chris asked. "I came to check on you since I left in a rush yesterday, is Cathy still here", Arnold said". "No, she's gone home, so how did your appointment go, were you able to see the person?", Chris asked. "Yeah, I saw her, it was a beautiful lady, uhm won't you ask me how I got in", Arnold said. "You know my password, it's no surprise you can enter, well I'd be changing it soon since I'm getting married in a few days", Chris replied. "Wow! So you've finally decided to settle down, who's the lady, is it Cathy or another person", Arnold said. "Do you know two ladies with me, it's definitely Cathy, I've known her for quite some time now and I find her lovely. We're registering our marriage on Monday", Chris replied. "That's so fast, but it's good you're getting married, what time is it", Arnold asked. "I don't know yet, but we'd be asked to pick a time since we're getting married in turns. You're coming with me", Chris said. "I'd definitely be there, congratulations bro", Arnold replied. "So, back to you, what's the gist", Chris asked. "The lady I met with yesterday, I really like her, her name is Mary, she's so cool and talented", Arnold replied. "Why don't you be with her since you like her do much, there's no time bro", Chris said. "I intend on confessing my feelings to her later on, we're similar in some ways", Arnold answered. "Bring her with you tomorrow, I wanna meet her, it seems you're real with this one", Chris said. We later went to Phoebe's place, she's Cathy's sister, her family is so welcoming, I can't wait to be part of them", Chris added. "Bro, you're doing well, I really envy you, Cathy is a great lady", Arnold replied. "So what's the new hit you're coming up with, I see you were rehearsing before you slept off", Arnold asked. "I'll tell you about it later, it's not meant to be disclosed for now", Chris answered. "Alright bro, have a drink with me", Arnold said. He went to Chris bar and took out some wines, they continued with their conversation before Arnold slept off at Chris place.

It was the next day, Cathy picked out a pant with fancy shirt for the dinner. She dropped it and thought it'd be formal, so she searched her wardrobe for an alternative and found one of the dresses Chris bought for her in a paper bag. She picked it and placed it on her body, looking at a mirror, and saw it was good on her, she found a matching heels in her shoe rack and decided to go with that. She rearranged her wardrobe, prepared something to eat, then took a nap. Arnold called Mary and asked whether she'd be available tonight. "I'm free tonight, what's up", Mary asked. "I'm having dinner with my friend tonight, he's coming with his fiancee, I don't wanna be a third wheel since I don't have a girlfriend to accompany me, so I thought you could do me the favor by going with me", Arnold answered. "Ohh that's the case, I'll go with you", Mary replied. "Thanks Mary, send me your address, I'll pick you by 8pm. I know you'll never disappoint me", Arnold said. "You're welcome, don't try to buy me with sweet words we'll talk later, bye", Mary said and hanged up.

Chris called Cathy and asked her to get ready that he'll pick her up soon. Cathy dressed up and applied lipstick, she styled her hair and wore a fitted gown with heels and waited for Chris outside. Chris arrived not quite long, he was mesmerized on seeing her. "You look sweet this way, I really admire you", Chris said. "It's the gown you bought for me, I'm glad you like it on me", Cathy replied. "I don't like the gown alone, I love you as well", Chris said and kissed her lips. Cathy smiled shyly, and said, "don't smear my lipstick, let's get going". "Who's more important, I or the lipstick, I forgot to say I like the lipstick too", Chris said. "You're shameless, how can you say such, you're the most important person to me", Cathy replied. Cathy and Chris went to the car and headed to the restaurant, Chris had texted the address to Arnold beforehand and said to meet by 08:30pm. Arnold picked Mary up at her place also, she was standing outside too, and was putting on pants and shirt, with heels. "You look gorgeous", Arnold said. "Thanks Arnold, I thought of putting on this since I feel comfortable in it", Mary replied. "Still, you're so beautiful, let's get going", Arnold said. Arnold left with Mary for the restaurant. Chris and Cathy got there before Arnold, a waiter approached them and asked if they made reservations earlier, or just wanna book a table. Chris replied they made reservation beforehand. "So what's your name", the waiter asked. "Donald Chris", Chris replied. The waiter looked at him and said, "you look familiar, wait you're the singer, Chris, is this your girlfriend, she's so beautiful and elegant, what's her name again, Cathy .. Kate, Kellie, I can't remember". "She's Cathy, my finances", Chris said. "Wow, we have a big guest here, your table is table 12, I'll take you there and make sure you're attended to well", the waiter said. The waiter called his colleagues, Chris was giggling him signal to stop, but the waiter was so full of joy. A waitress said loudly, "we have Chris in our restaurant here with his girlfriend". The people there drew closer to him and asked for his autograph, Cathy was thrilled, some took photos and videos, and uploaded it online. Everyone wanted to get close to him, Chris didn't know what to do anymore, Cathy held his hand and took him away, they found their table, it was a VIP's table in the dining hall, as there was enough privacy. A waiter came in afterwards and brought the menu. "I saw when Cathy held you, this is the menu, what would you like to order" the waiter said. Chris requested for wine and dessert, "Cathy will make the order when my friends arrive", Chris added. "Alright, I'll bring some appetizers too", the waiter said, and took his leave.

"So how did you know your way around here", Chris asked Cathy. "I've been here before on a work project, I happened to meet with the client in a VIP's dining hall, that's how I got to know my way around here", Cathy replied. "Ohh, that's it, the client must be very rich, hope he had no intentions by bringing you here", Chris asked. "No, he doesn't, he only wanted a private place to talk business while eating, besides I don't drink with my clients", Cathy replied. The wine and dessert was served, while they continued with their conversation. "That reminds me, do you drink Cathy?", Chris asked. "Yeah, I do, did you forget I once drank with a colleague in a bar, thanks to you, it didn't cost me my relationship", Cathy said. "James right, I remember now, you should drink with me alone from now on", Chris said. "Oh no, you're a jealous guy, you look so cute when you get jealous too, I won't drink with just anyone from now on. Arnold and Mary arrived at the restaurant, a waiter approached them and asked if they made reservations earlier, or just wanna book a table. "Donald Chris made a reservation already, we're dining together", Arnold replied. "Wow you guys are his friends, Chris presence caused an uproar earlier, everyone wanted to take a good look at him and get autographs. Thankfully, they don't know which dining hall he's in, they would have disturbed his peace. That's the advantage of coming to a top restaurant", the waiter said. "I thought it's only your food and services here that is great, I didn't know the workers here are great too, a lot of things has already happened, thanks to you, I get the gist", Arnold replied. "Thanks for your remarks, let me take you there, you see, Chris presence has brought more fame to our restaurant", the waiter said. They followed the waiter, Mary held Arnold's cloth and asked, "we're meeting with Chris and Cathy?". "Yeah, we are, is anything wrong, how did you know Cathy, wait, you may not even know her, Cathy is known as being Chris girlfriend", Arnold said. "Nothing's wrong, it's just so unexpected, let's go in", Mary replied. The waiter asked if they're going in, and they said yes, they went in. Mary and Cathy eyes met with each other, Cathy was surprised to see her, Mary was surprised as well, Cathy looked surprised too. "Excuse me, this is the menu, you can make an order", the waiter said. Cathy collected it and made an order for her and Chris, she passed it to Mary, and she made an order for her and Arnold as well. "What's going on, do you all know each other", Arnold asked. "Yeah, we do", Chris replied. "How did you get to know each other, you seem to be on good terms too", Arnold said. "We're on good terms, I and Mary used to work in the same place, she was my boss and recommended me for promotion, before she quit and began a career as an artist", Cathy said. "Is there any actual gist I don't know about", arnold asked. "It's not a funny thing, I thought Cathy was my love rival then, I was still so obsessed with James during that time, so I started disliking Cathy, it was later I found out she's dating Chris instead", Mary replied. "So, you actually disliked me because of a man, I can't imagine how many ladies would dislike me over Chris, so many girls are crushing on him", Cathy said. "I'm scared Chris", Cathy said to Chris while leaning on him. "Don't worry, you'll be fine, I'm always with you", Chris said while patting her. Cathy sat properly after that, their meal was served and they began eating. "I didn't know you could be a baby to Chris, see how you leaned on him", Mary said to Cathy. "I didn't know I could be that way too, his love changed me", Cathy replied. "I guess this dinner is a catch up for you ladies, you're leaving us out of the conversation", Chris said. "They're just rolling with each other, they'll make a good in-laws", Arnold said. "Sorry for leaving you guys out", Cathy said. Mary smiled and said, "Cathy, do you wanna know another reason I disliked you then". "What's the reason, I really wanna know it", Cathy replied. "I guess this is a confession night, how come you disliked Cathy alone without her disliking you", Chris said. "Well, I had always admired Mary's abilities and then strived to better", Cathy replied. "That's the exact reason I didn't like you then, you were better than me in the finance sector, you have good looks also, so I assumed you were my competitor", Mary said. They laughed over it happily, "it's really nice we can sit here together and have fun, Arnold should date Mary, no, he should marry her instead and make her my sister in law", Cathy said. "I didn't know when you started cracking jokes", Mary said. "You look pretty in your gown, it's my first time seeing you in one", Mary added. "Thank you sis, Chris got this for me to change my look. You look good in your outfit too, you're pretty", Cathy replied. "Wow Chris is more romantic than I thought, anyone can see his love for you", Mary said. "What do you mean by romantic, am I not romantic as well, Cathy said we should go out together, she's in support of our relationship. You can sense my feelings for you, I love you actually", Arnold said to Mary. "You guys would make a great couple, thanks for the remarks Mary, a good man knows how to care for his woman", Chris said to Cathy. Mary turned to Arnold and said, "do you have to confess your feelings for me here, aren't you afraid I'll say no, well I like you too". "Wow it's a couples night", Cathy said and made a toast to Mary and Arnold. She raised her glass and said "I wish you a happy relationship and mutual understanding". Mary and Arnold raised their glasses in turn and drank wine, Cathy drank hers too, Chris also raised his glass and drank. Mary proposed a toast to Cathy and Chris, she raised her glass and said, "I pray you grow old together and have lots of children". Cathy and Chris raised their glasses in turn and drank wine, Mary drank hers too, Arnold raised his glass also and drank wine. They laughed happily and talked about different things. It was 1000pm already, Chris said he wants to take his leave with Cathy, Arnold said he'd be leaving with Mary too, they bid one another goodbye and left.

Chris dropped Cathy at her house, "I had so much fun

today", Cathy said and hugged Chris. "I'm glad you did, I see you enjoyed your conversation with Mary too, you girls are matured, I'm proud of you", Chris replied. "Yeah I like Mary a lot, I'm happy she's with Arnold", Cathy said. "Will you be with me tonight, I don't want you to go", Cathy added. "You drank so much tonight Cathy, you should get some rest, we're getting married tomorrow, you'll move into my place if you want to and we'll hold a big wedding later on", Chris said. "I drank a lot because I feel happy and enjoyed your presence", Cathy said. Chris carried her, opened the door and placed on the bed in her room. "I'll be with you till you fall asleep, is that okay", Chris said. "Yeah it is", Cathy answered. She took his hand in her hands and fell asleep not long after. Chris couldn't bear to leave Cathy, so he removed his hand from her grip and slept beside her. Cathy touched the bed after Chris removed his hand, her eyes were still closed, she was looking for him, she was not deeply asleep, Chris held her close to him and pet her to sleep.

It was the next morning, Chris woke up before Cathy and prepared breakfast. Cathy woke up some while later, and sat on the bed. Chris entered the room and told her to freshen up. "You should shower now Cathy, so we can get prepared and leave home on time", Chris said. "I got you honey water, you should drink this first, you drank a lot last night", Chris added. Cathy collected the honey water and drank it. "Thank you Chris, I'll freshen up now", Cathy said. Cathy returned the mug to Chris and headed for the bathroom, while Chris returned to the sitting room. Cathy was done in the shower and put on a short with top. "You look good in everything, you should wear more of this", Chris said. "We should eat now", he added. "You've prepared breakfast already, I'm gonna wake up before you one day and prepare meal for us too, I can't let you do it everytime, thanks for the care", Cathy said. "It's alright sweetheart, I'm used to waking up early, I'll be looking forward to having your meal as breakfast, right, I'll be having your meal often soon", Chris answered. "So what'll will you be wearing today, you didn't go home last night", Cathy asked. "I have what to wear with me here already, what the both of us will wear, I bought it when we started dating newly, I took it along yesterday, I forgot to give you", Chris answered. "That's nice, you're so organized, thanks for everytime Chris", Cathy said. "Don't always say thanks, you should show it in your actions", Chris replied. Cathy kissed Chris lips for some seconds, and asked, "what about this". "Well this is more like it, you're getting me now", Chris replied. They ate breakfast and Cathy washed the dishes later on, they got dressed and heading out in a matching outfit.

WE MEET AGAIN

They got to the place and picked number 7, they were attended to not quite long and registered their marriage. Williams and Phoebe was waiting for them outside with gifts, Mary and Arnold was there as well with their gifts. Chris and Cathy came outside, his manager came to congratulate him, Phoebe and Williams congratulated them as well, together with Mary and Arnold. "How did you know about this", Chris asked his manager. "I got the news from a friend that works here and decided to surprise you", his manager answered. "Thank you so much" Chris said, hugging his manager. A few people were there to celebrate him, and some reporters were present too. "This is no longer a secret thing", Cathy said to Chris. "Yeah, it's just like I thought, but I'm happy", Chris answered. The reporters asked him when he'd be having a main wedding. "Your love for Cathy is so immense, when will you hold your wedding", a reporter asked. "You registered your marriage with Cathy, you must have a lot of plans together, but why didn't you announce it", another reporter asked. Chris held Cathy close, looked into her eyes, then smiled, he replied, "I love Cathy, I didn't announce my marriage registration because I didn't want to make her feel uncomfortable by the media pressure, and also thought of keeping this private, we'll be holding a wedding soon, thanks". Chris left with Cathy after then.

About The Author

Ojo Omolola Favour is a writer, speaker, and relationship advisor. She provides solid, practical answers and offers guidance in the areas of personal growth, singles issues, and relationships. She has helped many to achieve the love life they want and hosts relationship talks. Favour is available for seminars on a wide variety of topics, one on one counselling, conferences, educational events, and relationship talks. She is a lover of books, arts, and enjoys nature, currently residing in Nigeria, most likely multi tasking. You can reach out to her via her Instagram handle: @ojoomololafav

www.ingramcontent.com/pod-product-compliance
Lightning Source LLC
Chambersburg PA
CBHW031447150726
47990CB00007B/2649